BUMBLEBEE BOOKS
PARALYZED IN DREAMLAND

Raunak Agarwal is a storyteller and poet based in Kolkata, India. His first book, *Heart Broken Musings,* a first-of-its-kind Poetry/Rant motivational book was released in 2018 and was an instant bestseller.

One of the most popular bloggers on Instagram with over 50,000 followers, Raunak considers himself as a jack of all trades, who is slowly, but steadily working towards becoming the master of all of them. He is an avid dreamer and he often turns his bizarre dreams into funny, yet thoughtful short stories. When he's not writing, or dreaming, or making his readers swoon over his poetry, he runs a tax-consultancy firm along with his father.

To stay in touch with him, you can follow him on Instagram: @rk_writes95 or visit his website: https://raunakagarwal.com

BY THE SAME AUTHOR

Heart Broken Musings
The Things We Do for Love

Paralyzed in
DREAMLAND

- A Collection of Dreams -

RAUNAK AGARWAL

Published by Bumblebee Publishing
An imprint of Shree Balaji International
59, N S Road, 3rd Floor, Room No. 15B,
Kolkata, West Bengal – 700 001
www.raunakagarwal.com/bumblebee
Email: editorialbumblebee@gmail.com

Paralyzed in Dreamland
Copyright © Raunak Agarwal, 2020

ISBN Print Book - 978-81-944818-0-5

Although the author and publisher have made every effort to ensure the accuracy and completeness of information contained in this book, we assume no responsibility for errors, inaccuracies, omissions, or any inconsistencies herein. Any slights on people, places, or organizations are unintentional.

To everyone who has a dream, this book is a proof, that dreams do come true. (Sometimes literally.)

A NOTE TO READERS

Hi all!

Writing this book has been a dream project for me. After all, I literally had to sleep and see so many crazy dreams, before I could finalize on the fifteen dreams that I was going to turn into a book. And at times, this has actually made me question reality. For instance, there's a story in my book in which I dream about performing at an open-mic. Two days after I saw that particular dream, I went ahead and performed at my first ever open mic, but when I was done, I literally couldn't differentiate between the one I performed and the one I saw in my dream.

Doofus; the protagonist of the book, is loosely based on me. After all, Doofus is nothing but my subconscious, right? Just like Doofus, I used to be very smart in my childhood, but then, life happened, and things took a dumb turn. So, to find peace in this effed-up life, I think my brain created Doofus. So that, at least in my dreams, life is crazy good, for a change.

ΔΔΔ

CONTENTS

Based on Actual Dreams…

My Ex is Sorry?

R hea comes knocking at my door in the middle of the night, all stressed. Judging by her messy hair, smudged eyeliner, and an overly-sweaty face, it is obvious, she is drunk. This was something out of the blue! The last time I had seen her was around five months back, when I had decided to call it quits with her. Why? Because she was a lying shit-head who wanted the best of both worlds, while all I wanted was her. She had been conveniently cheating on me and that was something I could never tolerate.

She was so heavily drunk; she could barely stand straight. I brought her a chair and made her sit, trying to process the events in action.

'Is this a dream?' I asked her.

She began staring at me.

'Is this a dream?' I asked myself.

And, that is when my sub-conscious knocked hard at my sluggish brain and I began to panic.

• • •

'You have to take me back Doofus, I am sorry.' Rhea continued, 'I never realized how wrong I was. I know I've hurt you a lot and I am really very sorry about it. Please forgive me!'

I was bewildered. Since the day I had called it quits, I had been hoping for a scenario just like this. I always wished that one day she would come to my door and beg on her knees asking for my forgiveness. This was the closure my soul demanded, and I was finally getting it.

But was this for real? Had she finally come to her senses and realized that the guy she had been cheating on me with was nothing but a fuck-boy. Hell! He wasn't even rich; he was a fuck-boy with no money. Basically, he was just 'cheap'.

'Is this a dream?' I asked myself again.

All this while, she was still crying. She looked at me with googly eyes hoping I would say something. I stared back at her. A drunk girl and a sleepy guy, both with messed up eyes, continuously staring at each other. Oh! This was bad.

Just then, my father, who was sleeping in the room next to mine, woke up and shit got real. Rhea, dad, and I, were all now staring at each other. Oh, this was now turning into a nightmare.

To break this never-ending silence, I turned towards my father.

'She's Rhea, the girl I broke up with a few months back,' I said.

'Hi, uncle,' she said.

Well, why? My father hated the guts of her. He knew that she had made my life miserable and now, she just shows up at our house at freaking twelve am. My father was obviously furious. I have no idea what stuck his sleepy mind but he ran into the kitchen, took a jug of water, and poured it all over my laptop.

'Look what you made my old man do! Ok, now you owe me a new laptop,' I yelled, looking fiercely at Rhea.

You see, I belong to a typical Indian family. This means that me living with my parents is a normal thing – a symbol of our glorified culture. So, when I say that now my mom entered the scene, you should know that I am not a dumb-ass who still lives with his parents. Rather, I am just an ass and me living with my parents is a pretty normal thing.

My mom immediately tried to calm my father down but the damage was already done - I had already lost my beloved laptop.

I took Rhea to my room to ask her what had happened between that fuck-boy and her, and she began blabbering at the top of her voice.

Oh, what is it with women? Why do they think that yelling in a high-pitched tone is the only way to prove a point? At twenty past eleven, I had gone to bed with two perfectly functioning ears. Well, not anymore.

She kept blabbering for what seemed like another

half an hour. Generally, when women speak, it annoys the crap out of men, but here she was, all sorry and depressed, confessing about all her mistakes. Gosh! The more she spoke, the more I went into oblivion. Her words were like beautiful bullets to my now-defunct ears. Nonetheless, I finally asked her to calm down and go home because she was too effing drunk to remember anything that I would have said to her.

'Go home, you're drunk!' I said.

Just then, my mom budged into my room.

'Don't be so rude *beta*, look how drunk she is,' my mother continued, 'You should drop her home.'

Obviously, my mom was spying on us. Moms, you know!

'I drove here,' Rhea said.

And mom and I stared hard at the drunk woman.

'You brought your car?' I questioned.

She nodded.

I firmly held her hand and took her outside.

'I'll drive, I call dibs,' she said.

I stared at her hard. She stared back. I facepalmed.

Pee Pee Pee

I turned back to figure out who was honking his car this late and, lo and behold, it was Rhea's mother. She parked behind Rhea's car and began walking towards us.

Sla...

Rhea's mother tried to slap me. Hastily, I blocked

her hands and turned towards Rhea. She began to giggle.

'Hi mom, don't slap him, he's not the fuck-boy I told you about. He's Doofus,' Rhea plead.

Just then, my father who had been conveniently missing from all the action magically reappeared in front of us, but this time, with his lawyer friend, who also lived in our colony.

'Why? Dad, why?' I murmured.

Things were taking a legal turn now and well, that shit is fucked up. *Anything that goes legal is fucked up.*

Meanwhile, Rhea was busy trying to explain everything to her mother, to calm her down. I must say, despite her shortcomings, she has always been a mature girl. I mean, she was the one who was heavily drunk and yet, I was the one who had no idea how to handle this messed up situation.

I took a deep long breath and turned towards my father.

'It's all under control, let me handle it now. You can ask your lawyer friend to go back home,' I said.

My father looked at me and frowned.

Then, I turned towards Rhea.

'*Saara chutiyapa kisne kiya?*' I asked her. (Who was the fucktard who ruined your life?)

'Fuck-boy,' she murmured.

'*Sachha pyaar kisne kiya?*' I questioned her again. (Who was the one who truly loved you?)

'Doofus, you!' she said, in a low inaudible voice.

• • •

'*Aur tune dil use de diya? Kyun?*' I shouted. (And, yet you gave your heart to Fuck-boy? Why?)

Rhea was silent for she had no answer.

'Call me when you have an answer to this question,' I said.

I then looked at Rhea's mother and asked her to take her daughter home.

These past few hours had been super weird and I was glad that things were finally under control. And, to top that, my soul had finally got the closure it so deserved.

Despite our differences, I glanced at Rhea for one last time and smiled. And, she erupted in a never-ending curve of happiness.

'Nothing should ever happen between the two of you again!' my father said.

I looked at my father and nodded.

'Is this a dream?' I asked him.

My father nodded.

ΔΔΔ

The Werewolf

A small town: 11:48 pm.
Arh-Woooooooooooo

There was widespread panic amongst the hundred odd villagers because the inevitable was about to happen. The elderlies had been warning the parents of Doofus for weeks now. But despite all indications that it was time, the werewolf showed up at their village, Doofus had still not been able to decide his purpose in life. And now, it was too late.

The howl of the cruel monster coming from not so far away was a clear indication that it had arrived to take Doofus away, and no matter how much his parents tried, there was no way they could save him now.

A small group of villagers had gathered at the *village chowki* and were talking about the time when Doofus's father came to Ramakant's shop asking for all the holy things that were for sale.

'He took the Bible, the Geeta, and then he asked for the Quran,' Ramakant said, addressing the crowd.

'Poor fellow, he is a good kid, you know?' one of them said.

'Always smiling like some sort of lunatic,' another chuckled.

'At least they have his elder brother,' another one said.

Everyone nodded in acceptance.

They must have all been thinking about two years ago when the werewolf took away the only child of the *Sumra's*. Everything had been good since then. Even the kids had been very serious when it came to their goals and aspirations after that incident. After all, there was no greater fear than the fear of death. Even those kids who used to laugh it off as some sort of a folk tale had got their eyes opened when the incident had happened. But then, Doofus had always been one of a kind. He, for one, never believed that studies were his only chance at succeeding in life, and today he was going to pay the price for trying to break the rules.

Arh-Wooooooooooooo

'We've kept all the holy books at the door,' Doofus's mother yelled.

'And where is his brother?' the father asked.

'I've made Lore-master sit outside the front door with his favorite history textbook,' the mother said.

A tear rolled down the father's cheek.

'Don't worry, we won't let the monster take our Doofus away,' the mother mumbled.

'I am not worried about Doofus,' the father continued, 'I am just feeling proud about how much sincere our Lore-master has become.'

Arh-Wooooooooooooo

'The wolf is here… The wolf is here,' the neighbor's kid yelled, running across the streets.

Doofus's father returned to the drawing-room, calmly sitting on the sofa. He didn't care about the wolf. And after years of forcing Doofus to take his studies seriously, he didn't care about him either. But the mother wasn't one to lose hope. She quickly grabbed a *belan* (rolling pin) and stood outside the main door, locking it behind her. Doofus's brother was engrossed deep into his pointless studying. He would often say that he envied Doofus and his happy-go-lucky attitude, but he must have been feeling delighted at that moment. Funnily, his books didn't teach him that he was being used as a good bait to ward off the four-legged monster.

As for Doofus? He was there in his room, tied to the wardrobe with a thick set of red *dhaagas* (thread). The red *dhaaga* is considered auspicious in the Hindu culture, but considering that this was his father's idea, one may wonder if the *dhaaga* was for the good or for the bad of Doofus.

Arh-Wooooooooooooo

The wolf had finally arrived. It was a mighty beast

with sharp teeth coming out the sides of his drooling mouth. It was panting heavily, releasing pockets of foul smell with every breath. The wolf stopped right in front of Doofus's brother, sniffing him with a hint of pleasure. The mother could see it all, and even though she knew that the wolf couldn't touch Lore-master and nor could Lore-master see the wolf, she was frightened. In a panic, she hurled the *belan* at the werewolf.

It was widely believed that the werewolf would never harm anyone other than the one it was supposed to, but when the beast pounced at the mother, taking a sharp bite at her neck, all those beliefs were shattered. The villagers, when they later discussed all of this ruled that the werewolf thought that the mother was harming Lore-master. Who knows what the truth actually was?

It was only seconds before the mother fell to the ground, with blood oozing out of her neck, creating a pool of controversy.

The father, who was calmly noticing all of this from the window all this while, now rushed to his beloved's help. Surprisingly, he didn't call for Lore-master. Instead, he yelled for Doofus and that was all it took.

Doofus, who had no clue what was going down, heard his mother's scream followed by his father's call and a rush went inside of him. He gathered all his strength, breaking the thick set of red *dhaagas* that was wrapped around him and ran to where the voice of his parents had come from.

Doofus locked eyes with the werewolf for a split second, and the wolf howled proudly at the arrival of his prey, but before the wolf could do anything, Doofus rushed towards his brother.

Lore-master was a very tidy fellow and he didn't like it when his books got dirty, so he always used to cover them with some sort of self-healing cloth. Doofus snatched the book from Lore-master's hand, ripping the cloth off. He threw the book on the muddy ground and wrapped his mother's neck with the cloth. He then signaled at Lore-master to call the village Hakim. Finally, when he looked back up, towards the wolf, it wasn't there.

A week had passed since the incident, and even though, there weren't any more howls being heard, everyone was sure that the wolf would return for its prey. The learned had all been forcing Doofus the entire week to decide on his purpose. They wanted him to understand that he was special, and without a purpose in life, he was wasting this second chance that he had got. They even took Lore-master as an example of what he should be looking up to, but Doofus wasn't the one to budge. It wasn't that he didn't have a purpose in life, he did. In fact, he had many of them, but whenever he had tried to explain them to the people around him, they had all shut him off, and after years of unsuccessful attempts at trying to make people understand his desires, he thought, it was best to talk directly to the devil. That's when he had turned himself into a deliberate nut case.

Doofus knew that this wasn't over, and the werewolf was going to return. He even doubted that there was something much bigger behind this and his doubt was proved right, when the next day, the entire village was set on red alert for the celebration of MSG's arrival; the one who owned the wolf.

It was a day of grand celebration. All the villagers had taken out their cows and were bathing the cows with the purest of milk. As was the custom, MSG was going to arrive around noon, and before his arrival, the villagers had to do three things. One; to make sure that the entire village was drowned in milk, two; to make sure that all the cows were swimming in the milk, and finally three; to ensure that all the villagers were locked inside their homes. No one was supposed to come out until MSG left because if anyone dared, MSG would get them killed by the werewolf.

Normally, things would have gone as usual, but Doofus knew this was his chance, and he didn't care about dying or living, he cared about the answer, and with that in mind, a few minutes after noon, he jumped out his window in search for MSG.

Doofus wasn't exactly popular in the village, at least not for the right reasons, but over the course of his struggle, he had managed to make a few good online friends. And one such friend lived only a few miles away. It took quite a bit of convincing, but *Alternate Career* had eventually agreed to help Doofus out. Doofus met Alternate on the outskirts of the village and then they swam their way towards the center, where MSG was supposed to be.

It took a while to find him, and even after they did, all they could look at was a bright blob of white light shining in an unusual pattern. It wasn't sure if MSG was the light itself or if the light was shining out of him, and MSG didn't even give them time to ponder over it. He glanced at the two intruders and immediately signaled at the wolf to tear Doofus and Alternate apart. But Alternate wasn't a soft prey. Alternate hailed from a very progressive family. He quickly gathered a few facts inside his head, ultimately coming to the conclusion that werewolves didn't exist, at least not on Earth.

'You are not real,' he yelled at the top of his voice. He then looked at Doofus.

'Werewolves aren't real,' they both yelled in unison.

And just like that, the mighty beast vanished into thin air, taking with it all that light that was preventing MSG from being visible.

Doofus and Alternate turned towards MSG and were stunned to find what they were looking at. Because MSG wasn't a single person. MSG was a group of people, some related to Doofus, but most, unrelated to him.

Alternate turned towards Doofus and asked him, 'Do we say something or let them speak first?'

'Let's wait,' he exclaimed, 'Let's wait and find out… *Log kya kahenge.*' (What will the world say?)

And just then, all the MSGs started talking in a ruckus.

'Look he is friends with Alternate,' one of them said.

'We had one rule, and he broke it, he broke our tradition of not coming out during the festival,' another one said.

'He even challenged our strongly built *paramparas* by calling it not real,' another said.

Doofus's mother, who was also a part of MSG, rushed towards Doofus with a gleam in her eyes. Doofus thought she was going to hug him. Instead, she slapped him hard on his cheek.

'It's almost noon, wake up Doofus,' she said.

∆∆∆

The Girl Who Smiled

It was one of those days when, just like always, Utkarsh was sad. Being the flirtatious guy that he was, he had his eyes on almost every girl in our college, but this time, it looked serious. He asked me to meet him on the first floor near the restroom. This was one of those places in our college from where one could view the entire college campus. Although it was just a little over noon, many students were coming and going through the back gates. Soon, Utkarsh joined me and started his melodrama while I kept looking at the constant flow of students, all the while pretending to be listening to him. He had seen this girl near the green benches and was all pumped up about how beautiful she was; how beautiful her eyes were. He kept blabbering and I kept pretending.

'You used to be in a relationship with Rhea. You must know what love feels like, right?' Utkarsh asked.

This was a strange surprise. I have known Utkarsh my entire life and never had he ever blurted the word 'love' out of his mouth. From endless stalking on social media to creepy messages on WhatsApp, Utkarsh has never gone beyond that. And today, all of a sudden, he wanted to know how love feels? I was not going to buy it. But he wasn't going to let me go that easily. I looked back into the crowd.

'Nothing is better than the feeling of love. Even if it is in the past, the feelings will always stay. And when you stumble upon the person who used to be a part of your life, even if everything is over now, your eyes will flicker. The flicker is important… It says everything.'

Utkarsh gave me a weird look.

'What past? What feelings? I haven't even met her yet,' he frowned.

I facepalmed.

'Do you even know her name?' I asked.

'Yes, duh!'

'We go on our first date tomorrow.'

'Oh, wow!'

'And I can already see her as the mother of my child.'

Suddenly, I saw this girl coming into college through the back gates. I had never seen her before, but just looking at her face made my heart skip a beat. She looked up right towards me and surprisingly, she kept looking. We continued to stare at each other as I continued to explain love to Utkarsh.

'So, once the flicker ends, both of them will continue to stare at one another, not sure of what to do, the heads might move, but the eyes? They will stay stuck,' I said.

'You mean when I meet her, I need to look straight into her eyes?' Utkarsh questioned.

'Bang on,' I said.

The girl I had been staring at suddenly started looking up in the sky as she continued to walk slowly towards the main building and as such, towards me. She wasn't like one of those divas, you fall in love with at the very sight, and I could not explain my sudden rush of feelings for her, but something was surely there.

'The girl might feel shy, all girls do, and might look down or maybe up, but if you have feelings for her, if you feel a connection, you will keep staring, trying to express your emotions through the silence of your eyes.'

Utkarsh made a poker face at me. He threw his hands up in the air in disbelief.

'That sounds like a butt load of crap,' he continued, 'I'll take her out for drinks and then bang her brains out.'

'You sure?' I asked.

'Positive!'

'Really?'

'Umm… Okay! I'll take her out to this nice restaurant and then thank her for going out with me.'

'Attaboy!'

By this time, the girl had come very close. She

looked up again, only to find my eyes dead-fixated at her. Even she must have felt a connection because this time, she smiled, as she continued to walk towards the building and eventually faded from sight. Both of us never spoke a word, in fact, I had seen her for the first time, but there was a strange connection, a connection I could not explain. I thought of her again, and then I recalled her smile, and it immediately gave me the chills, because, in her smile, *I saw something even more beautiful than the stars.*

'That's my girlfriend you've been staring at,' Rahul whispered from behind, right into my ears.

And I immediately turned my head towards him.

'Is she new?' I asked.

'Yeah, her name's Naina and she's in the first year.'

'I am sorry,' I murmured, sticking my tongue out.

'Let's go *Doofie*, the class is over,' Utkarsh interrupted.

'What class?'

'*Rrrrrrriiiinng.*'

'What?'

'*Rrrrrrriiiinng.*'

'Whaat?'

'*Rrrrrrriiiinng.*'

'Whaaat?'

ΔΔΔ

Sam – The Ruddhi

'*Mumma*, I am ready,' I mumbled, wiping the tears off my face.

'Are you sure?' she asked.

'Yay,' I cheered.

'If you don't want to, you can go from tomorrow,' she said, not convinced by my sudden cheerful yes.

'But, it's the first day of my school *Mumma*,' I continued, 'I am supposed to cry.'

My mother gave me a stare, her burrows rising upwards in contrasting directions.

'You were acting all this while?' she asked.

I nodded.

My mother facepalmed.

'Who taught you all this, huh?' she asked pulling me closer by the ear.

'You did.'

My mother was about to say something, though I am not sure what, but then she paused for a second before speaking again.

'When did I teach you?'

'Remember… How in your wedding video, you start crying just before the *Vidai*?' I said.

'Hmm.'

'But then, moments later, the camera-man arrives, and you quickly wipe your face to pose for the *cam…*'

Before I could finish my sentence, there was a honk outside the door.

My mother, who was now looking at me with a flurry of mixed emotions, quickly held my hand. She then grabbed my school bag lying on the sofa and before the bus driver could honk again, she dragged me and my school bag outside towards the bus.

Giving me a tight hug, 'Talk to everyone on the bus, okay?' she mumbled into my ears.

As you already know, it was the first day of my school, and unlike what I had seen in all those cartoons, I was quite excited about it. After all, from now on, I was going to spend seven hours daily in this new place, and learn all kinds of new things… How could I not be excited? But then, right before I was about to board the school bus, my mother tells me to talk to everyone, and that's when I realized that, I wasn't ready for it.

Anyhoo, once the gates of the bus opened, I was greeted with this tall and slender woman who bent down, greeting me with a smile. She softly held my hand and helped me board the bus after which, she turned to my mother and started talking to her.

Once my mother and this woman who probably was also going to be my teacher were done talking, my mother waved at me one last time. The lady then held my hand again and guided me to the only empty seat on the bus. So, unfortunately, it wasn't a window seat as I was hoping for, and there was going to be another person sitting beside me, a girl.

'I should have stayed home,' I thought in my head.

As I continued to walk towards my pre-decided seat, I noticed that the girl was now staring at me. I don't know if she was the Cinderella type hoping that being the last to get a partner, she was destined for a prince or if she was an adventurous one, ready to make a prince out of a frog, and considering that she was looking at me with almost no facial expression, I really couldn't tell.

Once I was comfortable in my seat, the lady then walked to the center of the bus.

'Hello everyone!' she said out loud, but in a slow-paced and melodious way, making it sound like some song.

And in an instant, all the kids on the bus turned their eyes towards her.

'Now that everyone is on the bus, let's introduce each other, shall we?' she continued, 'I'll start… I am going to be your teacher, and while we are on our way to the school, you kids have to play a little game.'

'What game, miss?' one of the kids asked and then

raised his hands.

'You have to talk to the person sitting next to you,' she said.

Why? Why? Why? I was really looking forward to my first day at school. I was hoping that I'd go, learn some cool stuff, and then run back home to tell all about it to my mother. I didn't know I'd have to talk to other kids. It wasn't that I was an introvert or something. It's just that kids my age are generally dumb, and I didn't want to talk about dumb things with these dumb kids. I quickly glanced at my seat partner, who was still looking at our teacher. She was wearing a pink frock with her hair done the style of a ponytail. 'She'll probably talk about last night's episode of *The Power Puff Girls*,' I thought.

The teacher then walked up to her seat in the front and signaled at the bus driver to begin driving. But before sitting, she looked back again.

'Oh! And remember… You can only talk to a person for ten minutes and then you need to switch partners,' she said and sat down.

'I hope the bus ride is only for ten minutes… I cannot handle more than one *dum…*' I mumbled.

'Hi! I am Sam, *Sam - The Ruddhi*,' my seat partner interjected.

I looked at her and smiled without saying anything.

'Now, you tell me your name, duh!' she said and then began tracing her name on the fog of the bus's window.

'My name's Doofus,' I said.

Sam, who was busy tracing her name on the fog, now started tracing mine. She left a gap between her name and mine, and for a second, I thought she was going to draw a plus sign or maybe a heart, but instead, she drew a Moon.

'Don't you think that the Moon is heart-touching?' She asked, with her eyes fixated at her art.

This wasn't something I was expecting from her. I thought she'd ask the meaning of my name or maybe she'd ask about her window art, but she asked me if the Moon was heart-touching and I didn't know what to say.

'I don't know. It's just a Moon,' I said.

Sam instantly turned towards me. Her eyes were now wide with surprise.

'How can you not like the Moon?' She whined, grabbing hold of her bag below her seat.

At that moment, I thought that I was going to stay mum for the next ten minutes, but then I realized that she was also a kid like me, and if history is any evidence, she wasn't going to let this go unless I agreed with her.

By this time, Sam had taken out this fat book from her bag. She placed the book on her lap and then turned towards me as if she was still waiting for my answer.

'I like the Moon,' I said.

'Yay,' she said.

She then promptly opened the book which turned out to be a picture dictionary and showed me a photo of the Moon as seen from a telescope. And boy, was it beautiful!

'*Doofie*! Can I call you that?' she asked.

'Yup,' I said, excitedly staring at the Moon's photo.

'I often wonder about this universe of ours,' she mumbled, flipping through the pages of her book.

'Why did you flip the page?' I whined.

Sam turned the page back to where there was the Moon's photo and continued, 'I keep having this thought that if we like walked and walked and went beyond a certain point in the universe, we'd reach a place which had all the world's answer. Now, we'd not actually be walking since we would be in space, but it would be fun, right?'

I nodded.

She again continued, '*Doofie*, I had asked my mother once, if she knew what would we find if we looked behind the Sun, not too far, maybe just a few kilometers. And then my mother told me that the Sun was in fact in the center and this Earth of ours revolved around it.'

'That's why life goes a full circle,' I said.

She nodded.

'Since then, I've been reading about our solar system and everything beyond it,' she said.

'Wow! And what did you learn?'

'Not much, but I fell in love with the Moon.'

Sam then went back to her foggy drawing board and drew two more Moons, one beside each of our names.

There was something about her. Something that was urging me to make her a part of my life. She was definitely the adventurous type, and not just in a looking for a prince way, in fact, she didn't need to find a prince. She had the charisma, a mysterious essence, and if you were to consider her almost perfect ponytail, she was no less than a magical Unicorn.

'Why do you love the Moon so much? I asked her.

'Because it's there for us in our dark times,' she mumbled.

'So are the stars.'

'Yes, but they don't belong to our solar system.'

'Okay, so?'

'They cannot be trusted.'

I chuckled and shrugged my shoulder.

Sam immediately turned the page of her book to a picture of our solar system.

'Look!' she cried, 'Our Earth and all these other planets revolve around the Sun.'

'Yes.'

'But the Moon...'

'It revolves around the Earth.'

'Exactly! It cares for us. It's ready to absorb the sun's rays and reflect onto us even though it doesn't need it.'

'What about the Sun then?' I asked her.

'The Sun has other planets to look after. It can ditch us if it wants to,' she squeaked.

'Sam… You make no sense, alright?'

Sam gave a big frown and closed her eyes, and I knew she wasn't going to be the one to back down. I was waiting for her to just turn the page of her beloved book and make another scientific fact sound like something emotional… Something with a lot of unnecessary feelings.

'You think you're very smart, don't you?' she asked with her eyes still closed.

'Yup,' I said tilting my head right and back straight.

'Then you must know that it takes the Moon twenty-nine days to complete its lunar cycle…'

'And become a *Full Moon* again,' I said.

'And what do we do on that day?'

'I don't know.'

'Us women keep a fast for the safety of not-so-smart men like you,' she gushed and shut her book.

Okay! I was wrong. This girl wasn't mysterious. She was definitely not a Unicorn. She was just another emotional kiddo like other kids out there who was trying to justify her limited knowledge with the use of emotional feelings. But feelings are just feelings. They are not facts.

I thought about how I was going to challenge her and I realized that there was only one way to make her lose. I had to use my own feelings to defeat that of hers. But then I looked at her, and she looked so happy and bubbly. She didn't even care what I was going to say next, instead, she was back to drawing more Moons on the window, to a point that there wasn't any space left.

'Sam?'

She didn't respond.

'Sam – *The Ruddhi?*'

She turned towards me and nodded, though I wasn't exactly sure that she had heard me.

'You think I am dumb?'

For some strange reason, I had a hard time completing my last sentence, and even after I did, even though I was clearly audible, Sam didn't respond.

She did nod her head, but that was something she had been doing for a while now.

'*Joh bolta hai wahi hota hai,*' I tried yelling, but this time, I couldn't complete my sentence. (What one says is one himself.)

So, I tried to mimic it by pointing a finger at her, and then at me. But she just looked at me in confusion.

I tried to speak again, but no matter how hard I tried, the words just won't come out my mouth. I could hear everything in my head, and yet, none of it through my ears. Annoyed, I stood up from my seat and rubbed everything that Sam had drawn on the window.

But then I realized that I had done something

really stupid, so, I turned towards Sam, just hoping that she doesn't begin to cry. And luckily, she didn't.

Sam, who was patiently looking at me rub all her art, had a wide smile on her face. She gave her book a kiss and then handed that book over to me. I don't know why, but at the moment, I didn't feel annoyed anymore. I took the book from her and sat back on my seat. I wanted to say thank you, but words still weren't coming out from my mouth. So, as a gesture of my acceptance, I opened the Moon's page and began to trace my finger over it. But, when I looked back up, Sam wasn't there anymore. I looked around only to find her sitting with some other kid, tracing her name and the Moon all over again.

'She sure is mysterious,' I thought in my head.

As I continued to stare at her, I suddenly felt someone snatch my book from me. I turned around to figure out who it was, and just as I did, the mysterious person smacked the book hard on my head.

'Wake up *Doofie*... Or you'll be late for school,' my mother yelled.

ΔΔΔ

Naina's Rahul

Who was texting me this late? It was twelve am for god's sake. Nonetheless, I hurriedly rubbed my eyes and stared at the bright light coming out of my phone. It was Naina.

'Can you call Rahul once?' read her text.

Rahul! Age? Twenty-two. Gender? Male. Sexuality? Well, questionable!

Rahul was my best friend and Naina's boyfriend and Naina texting me to call him, after all, that had been going on between the two of us, meant only one thing; trouble.

'*Kya hua?*' I replied. (What happened?)

'He's feeling very low lately and is deeply disturbed by the fact that you won't talk to him… Can you please call him and cheer up his mood? Please?' she texted.

I didn't know what to say, but I am Doofus! Caring and hence, succumbing to people's wishes are the very ground rules of the yet-to-be-born Doofus generation. I took a moment to recollect everything in my sleepy brain and called Rahul.

*Like baby, baby, baby, ooh... **

'Hey! So, Mr. Doofus finally has time to call me?' Rahul exclaimed.

'Cannot see my young *Belieber* in a bad mood now? Can I?' I teased.

'Ha-ha, very funny.'

'Wait, I'll take Naina on conference,' I said and put Rahul on hold.

'Hello?'

'Why have you taken Naina on conference?' Rahul interrupted.

'She only told me to call you,' I said.

'No, I didn't,' Naina continued, 'Rahul... He's lying to you. I never asked Doofus to call you.'

Wait, what? Did she just say that? I looked at the wall clock staring at me. It was one am. I then looked at my cell phone, I was on a conference call with Rahul and Naina. I then looked at my other hand. I finally facepalmed.

I could have spent the next few minutes proving everything to Rahul with a simple WhatsApp screenshot or I could have simply chosen to sleep. But I was weak at making decisions, so, while my brain was stuck on a moral dilemma of either proving myself or falling asleep, my body dozed off.

'Wake up *Doofie*! Wake up now!' a voice shouted.

'Rhea… Is this you? I Love you too,' I murmured. (You guys remember Rhea, right?)

'What! It's me… Rahul,' the voice said.

I sprang up, startled, and stared at the unshaved face ogling at me. My room's window was open, and a gentle breeze blew right through the curtains causing the early morning sun rays to strike directly at us. I swear, if it was Rhea, I would have kissed her, but unfortunately, it was Rahul. My unshaved, bi-sexual best friend, Rahul.

'Where did you disappear yesterday? I… We were so worried about you when you stopped responding,' he said.

'I don't remember, but considering you just woke me up… I am pretty sure, I dozed off,' I replied.

'Get up and get dressed, we are going on a date,' he said.

'You and I?' I stammered.

'Yes… I mean, You, I and Naina.'

Rahul was staring at me with wide googly eyes, he had the same eyes I make whenever I look at a plate of biryani. This was scary and I was scared. I quickly grabbed my towel and ran into my washroom.

'Hello, Doofus! Long-time, no talk?' Naina shouted, waving at me from a distance.

I did not respond. Rahul waved back at her. This time, Naina did not respond.

• • •

Something smelled fishy, and the way they were reacting was only making things more complicated. The restaurant we were supposed to have our *dat*... Friendly meet in was a few minutes away. We walked in silence.

'Look there's a table, we can sit there,' Rahul said, finally breaking the silence.

It was one of those tables that's stuck to a wall and Rahul quickly grabbed the seat to the right of me. I looked at him amazed, and then I turned my eyes towards Naina with even more amazement while she moved towards the left one. There was exactly one seat left now, the one in the middle of the supposedly happy couple.

'We are definitely on a date!' I murmured to myself.

Both Rahul and Naina began to giggle.

'I am hungry,' Rahul said.

'Let's order a sandwich,' Naina said.

I rolled my eyes towards her. 'Haven't we already?' I exclaimed.

'No, duh! We just sat down,' Rahul said.

I looked left, towards Rahul, I then looked right, towards Naina. 'And people think I am stupid!' I thought in my head.

After a bit of confusion, we finally settled on two things; a sandwich and well, pancakes. Unfortunately, our order wasn't going to arrive for the next fifteen minutes, and I was done being stuck in this confusion.

• • •

'So, what is the deal with you two?' I asked.

'It's boring,' Naina said.

'Boring?' I said.

'I think we need to spice it up,' Rahul said.

'*Hain?*' I exclaimed.

Naina grabbed my hand and placed them on her thighs, making a rush of blood flow through my penis.

'You know Rahul likes to swing both ways, right?' Naina murmured, slowly brushing my hands over her pussy.

I looked at her in shock with my eyes wide open, and umm… a surprisingly large boner, but before I could react in any possible way, Rahul placed his hand on my boner.

'And I know you find Naina hot,' Rahul said.

'Yes… Wait, Nooooooo!' I stammered.

I quickly pushed Rahul's hand away and stood up. But then I realized that me getting up was only putting my ass in spotlight for both Rahul and Naina and that was a risk, I wasn't willing to take. So, I sat back down. I turned my head towards Naina, who was now smiling. Well, Rahul was right, Naina sure was hot. I placed my hand back on her pussy.

'This isn't real, right?' I asked.

'Doofus,' Naina cried, 'You and I are making a baby.'

'And then, I'll give you a colonoscopy,' Rahul added.

I immediately got up and grabbed a napkin.

Covering the bulge on my pant with the napkin, I rushed towards our waiter.

'Where's our *ord...*' I yelled.

'Sir, your room is ready,' he said, cutting me short.

He then turned towards our table and signaled a thumbs up. Rahul and Naina immediately got up from their seats and started walking towards us. The waiter then placed something on my hand, but judging from what I could feel, I was too afraid to look.

'Naina, what is all this?' I murmured, holding the Kohinoor in front of her face.

'Shush!'

Naina took the condom from my hands using her red velvety lips, and then dragged me towards the elevator. Rahul, who was now talking to the waiter didn't follow us. I couldn't hear much but the word butter did enter my ears, and right at that moment, I felt a chill down my spine. To calm myself down, I hugged Naina, tightly grabbing her firm tushy.

A moment ago, I was scared as hell, but once the warmth of her beautiful body embraced that of mine, and our heartbeats began beating in rhythmic sync, I could literally feel all my tension fade away. Now, I don't know if it was the lack of blood in my brain or the abundance of it in my penis, but I truly felt good.

'Babe! I am going to rock your world,' I whispered into Naina's ears.

She smiled. She reached for my hands, pulling them away from her tushy and we tip-toed into the hotel room.

'Close your eyes, *Doofie*,' Naina murmured.

I obliged.

Moments later, I felt the touch of those red velvety lips on mine. The exchange of saliva, the taste of her velvet lipstick, and the rush of kissing my best friend's girlfriend got so much into me, that except for my throbbing penis, I couldn't feel any other organ in my body.

Without opening my eyes, I quickly unzipped my pants, all the while kissing the patchy skin of Naina's cheek. *Wait, what?* And before my clueless brain could decipher anything, Naina gave me a swirl, and I felt a sharp pointy touch towards my back.

Startled, I opened my eyes, and that was the end of all that juicy build up that had led to my amazing erection, because, now I didn't have it.

'I've always dreamt of kissing you *Doofie*,' Rahul mumbled from behind, brushing his bi-sexual penis against my body.

I immediately got up and took a step away from him, scanning the room for Naina.

'You really thought you were going to have sex with my girlfriend?' Rahul asked.

I didn't know what to say.

'Where is she?' I asked.

'In the other room, probably masturbating from all the horniness you built into her.'

'But... But?'

'It's okay best friend, I am here for you,' Rahul continued, 'Come to daddy, will you?'

Scared, I rushed towards the door, but it was locked.

I don't know if the hotel walls were thin or if I actually made Naina a tad too horny, but I could hear her loud moans. And, so could my penis.

'Look who's finally ready,' Rahul exclaimed.

'But I am not,' I pled, 'Please Rahul… I am not gay.'

'*Doofie*! Are you ready?'

'I am sorry, I grabbed Naina's tushy.'

'*Doofie?*'

'I am sorry, I kissed her red velvety lips.'

'*Doofie?* Open the washroom door.'

'…'

Rahul tried opening the door. Surprisingly, it was open. He rushed inside to find Doofus sitting on the commode, restlessly sleeping. He started shaking him vigorously, and as soon as Doofus opened his eyes, he began laughing.

I fainted.

ΔΔΔ

Dhongi Baba Mandir

I've been an inseparable part of my family for almost twenty-two years now, and as it goes with all families, we have certain customs, and when it comes to these customs, we take them very seriously. Now, I wouldn't call myself an atheist, nor would I consider myself as someone who is deep into religion and stuff, but then, I am a stupid person, living a stupid life in a perfectly stupid world… The heck do I know?

'But I don't want to,' I frowned, looking down at the floor.

'It's a good place and you'll love it,' my colleague interjected.

'They say, the place is full of miracles,' my father added.

'And all your wishes come true over there, right?' I asked, mockingly.

'Only if you go over there with a pure heart,' my colleague said.

'Umm…'

'You are coming with us,' my father said, in a low, and yet, assertive voice.

And, that was how my father and my colleague convinced me into going to this *Mandir* (Temple) with them. In their defense, this was no ordinary place. This *Mandir*, as my colleague had been blabbering about, was an hour's drive from our office, and was situated amongst the lush greens of the Sundarbans. And as it turns out, my colleague was a member of the committee at the *Mandir*.

'He must be getting a hefty commission for taking us,' I mumbled to my father.

He didn't respond.

'You will love the drive,' my colleague continued, 'It's got all these castles and palaces, and the road's all curvy.'

'Yeah, yeah,' I murmured, 'So, what do I enter in my navigation?'

'*Dhongi Baba Mandir.*'

I looked at my colleague with astonishment. I, then, turned towards my father. But, once I saw him grooving to a bhajan of the very same *Dhongi Baba,* I knew there was no point in talking about it.

My father, who by now, was totally engrossed into this *Dhongi Baba's* tunes, quickly took the front seat, not wasting a second in connecting his phone to the car's speaker. My colleague was going to drive, and he got inside as well. Sensing that this trip was inevitable,

I opened the car's back door and just as I was about to enter, my colleague fired up the engine causing the annoying bhajan to blast right into my ears.

I looked at my colleague, giving him a blank stare, but he just smiled. He then moved his hand towards the volume button which for a second did make me happy, but then he turned it up a notch, and with that, my happiness instantly drowned into the pool of unwanted noise.

Despite all the disappointment that this trip was going to be, my colleague was right about one thing, the drive – It was freaking awesome.

It was a clear day, with a hint of clouds in the sky. The sun wasn't too bright, and the winds were flowing heavily. This was as perfect a weather as it could be. The lane that we were driving through was a one-way road, which to me looked quite suspicious. Well, for one, we were going uphill, and secondly, this was supposedly a very famous place. And if so many people were going uphill through a one-way street, how were they even coming back down?

For a moment, I was curious, but as I ogled at the beauty of the hills, at the lush greens, at the small cottages that were slowly turning into ant houses, I could see myself lose touch of reality.

'This trip isn't half-bad,' I thought to myself.

And just when I had thought this, we reached our destination or were supposedly about to, because my colleague took a sharp right towards one of the VIP parking areas, bringing the car to a complete halt. A few meters away from us was the line for the entry. It was a standard zig-zag styled lane to effectively control the crowd, and as I continued to scan through the location, I noticed the board that read: Ticket counter. To my surprise, my father was already there and was in the process of taking those tickets.

As is customary, we opened our shoes and joined in line waiting for our turn to look at the holy figure. I don't know why, but as we were getting closer, I had a strange feeling, I was getting moody, lost in pointless thoughts, and the black and red hues of the *Mandir's* walls were setting the perfect tone for all my crankiness.

'So, you liked it?' my colleague said, interrupting my thoughts.

'Liked what?' I asked.

'The holy deity? Isn't it magnificent?'

I stared blankly at him for a while, then I turned my head around towards our line, only to realize that we had already exited the main area.

Embarrassed, I nodded at him and smiled.

'So, how do we go back home?' I asked, with a bit of disappointment for not being able to have a look at the deity.

'We don't.'

'Okay… Excuse me?' I blurted.

He didn't respond. I turned towards my father, hoping for some kind of reaction, but he didn't

• • •

respond either.

I swear, at that moment, all the suspicions, all the uneasiness, were trying to jump into devious conclusions. And just when I was about to declare this place as some sort of a messed-up cult, my eyes fell on the board that read exit, and I calmed my judgments down.

As we reached the exit, we were stopped by a bunch of color-coded people. From what I could interpret, they were members of this place. They asked my father for the car keys, which he happily gave them. Then one of them escorted us towards the office beside the exit.

'They have valet here?' I asked, quite surprised.

Bam

My father smacked my head. 'Mind your words, *Doofie*,' he said.

'Your father gave the car in service of the holy God,' the color-coded man spoke.

'Dude?' I yelled.

'What?' All three of them said, staring right at me.

'We drove up-hill, how will we go back down?' I mumbled.

'We'll walk,' my colleague said.

And so, we did. We walked and walked and walked, for the next thirty minutes. I swear at one moment, we came across a skeleton and instead of being alarmed about it, we just jumped right through it, straight onto the spiral exit, until we reached

• • •

another gate.

And on the other side of the gate, wasn't freedom. Rather, it was the same *Mandir*, only a shade darker. This was fucked up, and not even in a *chalta hai way*. This was some other level sorcery that my colleague had put us in, and I had to somehow break my father and myself from it. Now, I knew that questioning this situation would only make it worse. I had to play at this game instead. I could see our car, a few meters from us. I could also see my father walking towards the ticket counter.

I quickly grabbed my father's hand, stopping him from moving forward.

'It's a good place and they'll love you,' I said, looking at my colleague.

'They say, the place is full of miracles,' my father added.

'And all your wishes will come true if you bring new people to them, right?' I said.

'Only if you go over there with a pure heart,' my colleague said, with a bit of hesitation.

'You are coming with us,' my father said, in a low, and yet, assertive voice.

'Yes, dad!' I continued, 'And if we don't hurry, we'll be late for our office.'

I noticed that my colleague had my father's phone and was trying to open the music player on it.

'Don't we have to call this client urgently? He owes us a hefty commission,' I said, quickly snatching the phone from my colleagues' hand.

'You will love the drive,' my colleague continued, 'It's got all these castles and palaces, and the road's all curvy.'

'Yeah, yeah,' I murmured, 'So, what do I enter in my navigation?'

'Doofus Incorporation,' my colleague said, handing my father the car's key.

'Doofus…' he repeated.

Bam

'Wake up, Doofus,' my father yelled from outside the window of his car and then, went on walking towards the ticket counter.

ΔΔΔ

Bhai Ki Shaadi

Bhoooshook

'Why did you do that?' my mother continued, 'They are your brother's in-laws for god's sake.'

My mother was right. No matter how much I loathed being dragged to my cousin brother's wedding, throwing *Badam halwa* (A sweet made of Almonds) at his in-law's window wasn't a gentlemanly thing to do. In fact, who in his right mind would ever do that?

'I am sorry *maa*,' I murmured, putting my head down.

Just then, my father and a few of our relatives came rushing towards us. My father tightly gripped my hand, dragging me towards the community room of the hotel, a place, where all the serious decisions concerning the wedding had been taking place for the past week. My mother quietly followed suit.

When we reached there, my cousin was sitting on

a chair, in one of the corners. I don't know why, but I felt a chill go down my spine.

'Here he is,' my father yelled, pushing me right into the center.

My cousin glanced at me and shook his head away.

'Umm?' I murmured, scanning the entire room.

The bride, who was standing just a few meters from me, looked at me and winked.

'So, we've been talking,' the bride's father said.

'And what you did…' my father said.

'Was tasty,' the bride said.

'I am *sorr… Wait, what?*' I gushed.

'Sasu ma tells me, you cooked it yourself?' she continued.

I glanced at my mother in confusion. She smiled.

'Yes,' I said.

The bride slowly walked towards me, stopping right in front of me. She was so close; she was literally breathing on my face.

'*Doofie,*' she whispered, 'I know I am your brother's fiancée.'

'Yes…'

'But after having that *halwa*, I can't stop thinking about you,' she mumbled into my ears, giving me a tight hug.

I swear, at that moment, I felt like hanging myself out of embarrassment, but after thirty seconds of easing into the warmth of my brother's forbidden fruit, I couldn't care less. I let go of all my inhibitions

• • •

and hugged her back, pressing my chest, tightly against her.

'So, *Doofie*, will you marry me?' She asked.

'Omg! Yes,' I yelled, in excitement.

But then, I realized, I had just agreed to marry my brother's fiancée, in front of an entire army of judgmental relatives, and well, the former groom, my cousin brother.

I kissed the bride's forehead and turned towards my cousin, but he wasn't there. I then scanned the room again, and to my surprise, everyone looked happy.

'I've saved some *halwa* for the honeymoon,' the bride murmured, and quickly left the room, making way for all the *aunties, bhabhis* and my sisters to pamper the new groom; me.

The next day

Knock Knock

'Doofus? You there?' a familiar voice yelled from outside the room.

It took me a second, but once I recognized the voice, I couldn't have been sadder.

I opened the door. 'Hey, you made it,' I said, in a grumpy voice.

'I had to! It's my best friend's cousin's wedding, after all,' Rahul gushed.

'Umm… Actually, it's mine.'

'Whaaaaat?'

'I know, it's sudden, but…'

● ● ●

'But the e-vite said it was your cousin's wedding.'

'Yes, and yet you are here, a thousand kilometers away from home, based on a freaking e-vite,' I frowned.

'Oh! You can't get married without your best man being there.'

'I guess.'

'So, where's Rhea?'

'What? Rhea is here?' I asked, astonished.

'Rhea is not here?'

'Why would she?'

'Omg! That's why you sent me an e-vite,' Rahul continued, 'It's an e-wedding!'

'Dafuq? It's a normal physical wedding and Rhea is not the bride. My cousin's fiancée… I mean his ex-fiancée is the bride.'

Rahul looked at me blankly for a good two minutes. Then, all of a sudden, he started laughing.

'I know it sounds crazy, but she liked my *halwa*,' I said with a bit of embarrassment.

'Dude! You cannot do this to Rhea.'

'Rhea doesn't love me anymore.'

'And you certainly cannot marry someone else's fiancée because she liked your *halwa*.'

'Also, my father hates Rhea.'

'Wait, *halwa* the sweet or *halwa* the hanky-panky?'

No matter how happy I was about getting married, the fact that I was giving up on even the slightest chance of getting back with Rhea had not hit

• • •

me, until now.

'Screw this,' I thought in my head.

'Where are you lost?' Rahul asked, waving his hands in front of my face.

'Nothing… I think I was daydreaming,' I said.

'Are you sure?'

'What do you mean?'

'It's six in the evening,' Rahul continued, 'And you need to get dressed. I brought a Sherwani for you.'

'Gosh! Daydreaming is not time-specific,' I muttered, taking the Sherwani from Rahul's hands. I then signaled him to leave.

'If you say, I'll call Rhea right now and we can change the bride just the way you changed the groom,' he said before exiting out the door.

What is it with villages? You take an open land, dress it all up in fancy clothes, garnish it with a bunch of beautiful flowers, fill it with people wearing a variety of imported perfumes, and the place will still smell like cow dung. So, how could my wedding be an exception? There were two aisles of chairs, facing towards the mandap. On the right-hand side of the mandap was the food area, where unlike other weddings, the guests were being made to sit cross-legged, while the traditionally dressed waiters served food on their plates. And, in the center of the mandap were the bride's parents, eagerly waiting for their daughter's arrival.

As I entered the ground, all the sisters and the

sisters-in-law's came rushing towards me, taking turns at getting that perfect selfie with the not-so-perfect groom. And it was only after thirty minutes of smiling and pouting, that I was finally allowed to join my mother at the *mandap*.

'Where's the former groom?' I jokingly asked.

'Shush!' my mother continued, 'He's off drinking in some bar, I guess.'

'Shit! Seriously?'

'Yeah, Rahul took him.'

'Perfect. After being left by his fiancée, a bi-sexual drinking partner is what my cousin needs,' I thought to myself.

'And where is my beautiful wife-to-be?' I asked my mother.

'I don't know, probably getting makeup.'

'*Rukooooooooooo,*' (Stop) Rahul shouted from a distance.

There was a car behind him, and from what I could see, there were three people inside; my cousin brother, my future wife, and a semi-nude guy sitting in the front.

'Oh! He didn't,' I said and facepalmed.

My cousin opened the car window and peeked out. He had a subtle smile on his face for some reason. Meanwhile, Rahul rushed towards the *mandap*, immediately pouring a bottle of wine in the *Agni-Kund*.

'Dafuq, you doing?' I gushed, pushing him away.

'I am putting off the fire,' he stammered.

'Really? With wine?'

'Oops,' he continued, 'Wait, I'll pee on it.'

Smack

My father registered his hand on Rahul's face.

'*Rukooooooooooo,*' (Stop) my cousin shouted, from inside the car.

He firmly gripped his ex-fiancée and my beautiful wife-to-be's hand and dragged her towards us. Halfway through their slow-motion dramatic walking, the semi-naked guy rushed out the car, and ran away, without even looking back, as I continued to stare at the entire incident in utter confusion.

'Did none of you notice that the bride was missing?' my cousin asked.

And what followed was a unison of murmurs among the entire crowd.

I looked at my wife-to-be and she looked stunningly beautiful, but then I noticed her dress, and the entire attire looked rushed up. Her blouse was missing a button, her saree was uneven, and her bra, well, for some reason, it was hanging out the sides of her waist.

'What happened to you Rhe… Wait!' I continued, 'I don't even know my wife-to-be's name.'

Rahul, who was covering his face with one hand, lifted the other hand, signaling a phone call towards me.

'Ugh! The name's not important. Whatever

happened to you? Who was that semi-nude guy?' I asked.

She didn't respond, trying her best to look away from the curious and judgmental crowd.

'We found her at the bar with that guy who just ran away,' my cousin yelled, addressing the crowd.

'And we caught her enjoying that guy's *halwa*,' Rahul added.

My cousin's mother, who all this while had been strangely missing from the scene, started yelling at the top of her voice until my mother confronted her.

'How could you?' I said, in a soft inaudible voice.

'Because, I was dead sure that you will say no to me,' she continued, 'Who even agrees to marry his cousin's fiancée?'

'But… You liked my *halwa*. You even hugged me. You are so beautiful.'

'And also, out of your league.'

The murmurs were getting louder by the second, and so was the embarrassment on my face. And to add to that, my cousin was simply standing there and laughing, like a weirdo.

'This wedding is off,' I yelled, throwing a fit.

I turned around to run away from the scene, only to be stopped by Rahul, who swiftly handed me his phone.

'Rhea's on the line,' he gushed.

'H… Hi!' She exclaimed.

'Hi.'

'What you doing?'

'Getting married,' I said, in a cranky tone.

'I know that stupid, but that's off now, right?'

'Umm… Yes.'

'So, what are you doing now?'

'Rhea,' I cried, 'Come back in my life, again, please.'

'I will.'

'Really?'

'In here, yes. Out there, no.'

'What do you mean?'

'*Doofie?*'

'Yes, my love?'

'You love me?'

'Yes, my love.'

'You miss me?'

'Yes, my love.'

'You want to win me back?

'Yes, my love.'

'Then, wake up!'

Yes, my… Wait, what?'

ΔΔΔ

Award Goes To?

It was a long tiring day and even though it was already past eleven, I still had a ton load of work to do. Realizing that my body could no more cope with the adversaries that my job required, I decided to stop and head for my home, to my beloved wife; *Pornhub*.

'Even the janitor must have gone home,' I thought in my head.

I exited the main building and rushed towards the top floor of the parking wing to get my car. *A white matte colored, top of its class, four-seater beauty; my Ambassador.*

I had just entered the parking wing when I realized that I was being followed. I did not really have the courage to look back, but from what I could see in the shadows, the person appeared to be holding an axe or something. Afraid, I began to sprint.

One floor. Two floors. Three floors. I ran.

One floor. Two floors. Three floors. The shadow

followed.

I reached the top floor only to find the stupid door closed and bam! I almost shit my pants. I was continuously shaking my head left and right, all the while cautious of the devil in the shadows when I noticed the unlocked janitor's closet. I ran for the closet in an attempt to hide inside it, when suddenly, from nowhere, the janitor arrived and unlocked the door to the parking wing.

Now, a normal person would have stopped and taken help from the janitor, but I was stupid. Normal never really translated to me.

I totally ignored the janitor and rushed towards the now open gate. I remembered that the car was parked on the right side of the gate, but taking a straight right would have been so obvious, right? So, I took a left, to circle around the floor and try and fool the devil; the devil with the axe.

Just as I was about to reach my Ambassador, I saw another car about to exit the premises, and me being me, I cooked up another crazy idea inside my head.

'Okay, this car just left. What if I hide here itself and let the devil think that I took the exit? He doesn't have my number plates, anyway. Wow, I am smart. I wonder why my mother named me Doofus,' I mumbled to myself.

Innnstagrammmmmmmm!

There was a loud thudding noise, but the sound of that noise was different. And, that's when it hit me.

Just yesterday, I had had a telepathic talk with God, boasting to him about my successful page on Instagram and all the lovely followers I had there. I had also challenged him that no-one, not even he could make me part with my beautiful page. And I am pretty sure he took it on his ego.

'This was no devil with the axe. This was God, maybe Shiva; the destroyer,' I thought.

I could now hear the Devil/God closing in on me. I confided to one of the corners and curled myself like a ball, anxiously waiting for my fate to hit me with the axe of ego. The footsteps were getting louder with each passing second.

One step. Two steps. Three...

The Devil/God grabbed me from behind.

'Congratulations! Here is your Trophy,' the Devil/God said.

'Please don't kill me,' I whined.

'Welcome to *"Instagram Dreams"* where passionate people are tested,' the Devil/God continued.

'Whaaaat?'

I opened my eyes in wide bewilderment to find an entire army of bloggers, writers, comedians, feminists, and the so-called *Influencers,* clapping with immense joy and excitement. I stood up, amazed, but at the same time, shocked.

The Devil/God whom I could now clearly see was not what I had expected. It was a normal human being, a white-coated scientist, and what he was holding wasn't an axe, but a trophy.

'We are the people of *Instagram Dreams* and we test passionate Instagrammers in bravery, valor, strength and their uniqueness.'

'Umm… Okay,' I said.

'Those who pass get on the favored list of the Instagram algorithm, and those who fail are stripped off their Instagram accounts,' the scientist continued, 'The uniqueness with which you handled the entire situation had us all amazed and we are happy to tell you that you have passed the test.'

'Yay,' I yelled.

'Take this trophy. Now, would you like to say a few words?' The scientist asked.

I was awestruck! Was this for real? Were my struggling days over? Would I finally be getting tens of thousands of likes on all my posts? I had so many questions in my mind, I wasn't sure where to begin. Anyway, I received the trophy from the fine gentleman and cleared my throat for the speech.

'I, Doofus, from the famous Instagram page *rk_writes95…*'

'Wake-up *Doofie*! It's almost twelve!' a voice that sounded like my mother's yelled.

I rubbed my eyes hard only to find my mother staring at me with anger and disappointment.

'Get up and get dressed for college,' she said.

I shook my head, confused. Finally realizing that

all that had been happening a while ago was nothing but a mirage, I got up from my bed to get ready for college.

'No wonder, my mom named me Doofus,' I frowned.

The God's photo on my side-table had a strange kind of smile.

I frowned again.

ΔΔΔ

Heart-Ball

'Mother, I am excited,' I said, waiting in line outside the Cupid's chamber.

'Calm down, it's not like you are going to find your true love straight away,' my mother mumbled.

'I know,' I cried, 'But I am finally getting my very own Heart-ball... And after listening to so many stories from dad, I can't wait to find my soulmate.'

My mother looked at me and shrugged. She then started telling me about how many tries and re-tries my father had gone through before he finally set his eyes on her. And even then, she said, it took my father at least three more deaths before he could convince her for marriage. Deep down, even I knew that it wasn't going to be easy, but I was embarking on an adventure of my own, and no matter how scary it was going to be, I was truly looking forward to it.

La la la la, la la... Excitedly, I began humming.

A week later

'Is it true? What they say?' Utkarsh asked, circling his fingers around the ball that was tied to my neck.

'About?' I asked, looking at his movements, afraid that he might just pull the string out any moment, just for fun.

'That if I break this, you'll like… *Die?*'

'Yes,' I continued, 'And respawn in some other part of the world.'

'And how do you know that you haven't been respawned before?'

'Because the memories don't go… They stay.'

'It's sick… You know?'

'Oh, beat it. Even you cannot wait for your own heart ball.'

Utkarsh didn't respond. But I knew he was asking all these questions because he was due for his heart ball in a couple of days, and he wanted to boast in front of all the ladies who were going to be there, by knowing everything already. Even I didn't mind telling him all of this, after all, what Utkarsh didn't know was that women were allowed at the Cupid's chamber only after they had chosen a soulmate.

I looked at him and smiled widely.

'You know,' I continued, 'I keep having this dream…'

'What sort?' Utkarsh questioned.

'Like, all of this, this world of ours… Somehow, we are trapped in it, and there's this one way, we can break from it and go into the real… The actual world.'

● ● ●

Just then, my mother came in to ask Utkarsh if he needed something to eat. And by the time she was gone, we were back to adoring my Heart-ball.

Around an hour later, when it was finally time for Utkarsh to go back home, he came close to me and whispered in my ears:

'I've heard… If your heart ball dies, you are dead forever?'

'Yes, but only if someone else destroys it.'

'What if we destroyed it ourselves?'

'I don't know.'

'Hmm.'

It has been around two months since Utkarsh and I had this conversation, and since then, he has respawned five times already. Last time I heard from him, he was in some western country, mating with women after women. He said he was going to drop the very idea of finding a soulmate because he was enjoying the entire western culture way too much. He said he had already rejected three women after he managed to sleep with them. Knowing him, this kind of behavior wasn't much surprising, but even he knew that this couldn't go on forever. The Heart-ball was a delicate gift, and if Cupid ever found out that he was misusing it, he could have his ball taken away, and they say that nothing good happens after you lose your ball.

Anyway, enough about that poor fellow. As I said, it has been two months, and boy, my life has taken a turn for the best.

I am not supposed to be telling this, but that day, when I had gone to the Cupid's, you know, to get my very own Heart-ball… One of the ladies out there was none other than the royal princess. She looked at me, and I don't know if it was some *what's destined shall find its way* sort of thing, but at that exact moment, the boy she was going to spend her life with, had a moment of weakness, and he respawned. So, long story short, I was going to marry the princess. Now, don't get me wrong, I was very happy about this, but then, I hadn't respawned even once, and if things were to go like they were, I wasn't going to respawn ever, and even though it wasn't exactly a good thing, everyone wants to experience it, right? It's magical, and no one ever says *no* to magic, right?

Another thing was that, even though the princess had set her eyes on me, and I, on her, we weren't going to be like other normal soul-couples. She was a princess, after all. And as it goes with all royal matches, I had to compete in a *Swayamvar* and be officially declared as the soul-mate for her. And, when my lady told me about this, I'll admit, I got really nervous because I wasn't good at competing. I was barely good at living, and to convince a bunch of royal people that I was going to be able to give my lady a beautiful life, wasn't going to be an easy job to do.

'*Doofie,*' the princess mumbled, 'You love me, no?'

This was after we had finished having hours of

vigorous sex, and we had been too tired to dress back up. So, we lay naked beside each other, taking in the warmth of our bodies, and making it our own. Obviously, I loved her, and not just because she was beautiful and a princess… I loved her because she resembled a tad too much like the girl I kept seeing in my dreams, much before I had met my lady. Yes, the same girl who would tell me that this world of ours wasn't real. There was a certain kind of charm in the princess, the sort that entraps you into a sweetness like no other, but as I said, this was after we had had hours of vigorous sex, so maybe I was tired, or maybe I was simply unconscious, but I didn't respond.

And the next thing I remember was, I woke up in my bed, only this one was a bit different. No, not different… It was freaking huge. I looked around, trying to consume myself into how huge my room was, until, it finally dawned onto me that my lady had broken my Heart-ball's string and I had respawned as a prince; The prince of *Revada*. It wasn't like we were given a manual or something for our new lives, but maybe, somehow, all our respawns, all our deaths, were decided the very day we got our Heart-ball, and maybe, just maybe, we had all this information in our subconscious from the very beginning, waiting for the right moment. Because, I had just woken up, but I knew everything about my current life as well as the old one. I'll admit, it made me nauseous at first, but once it hit me, that I was now a prince, I couldn't wait to tell my mother and Utkarsh about it. But I didn't know where Utkarsh was, so, I called my mother.

Ring Ring Ring

'Hello,' the voice from the other side spoke.

'Hey, mother… You wouldn't believe where I am,' I yelled, in excitement.

'I am sorry, who's this?' my mother questioned, puzzled.

And that's when I realized why respawning was a bad thing. It lets you keep your memories, but it also takes away the very same memories from anyone connected to you.

'But, Utkarsh remembered me, didn't he? And I still remember him…' I mumbled.

'It only affects blood relations,' the butler spoke from behind, completely startling me.

'You're our one-sixtieth prince, and the third one this week,' he continued.

'Umm… Wow!'

'And normally, I'd let you enjoy your stay while you can, but we need to leave now,' he said.

'Where?'

'*Neelavari…* There is a…'

'*Swayamvar,*' I said, cutting him short.

'Yes. How did you know?'

I thought for a second but eventually decided against telling him anything.

'I just know,' I said.

It took us around eight hours to reach there, and

• • •

even though I was excited about how destiny had brought me back to the same place, I was going to spend my life at, I couldn't help but think of my lady and how she was going to react to see me there, only this time, much more worthy of being called her King.

We were taken to our chambers and were briefed with all the proceedings that were going to take place the next day.

'When can I see the princess?' I asked the briefer.

'Your Highness,' he continued, 'Things haven't been great since our princess lost two soulmates, so it was decided that this was going to be a blind *Swayamvar.*'

'As in?'

'You cannot see her unless you are chosen.'

'But... I am.'

'You are?'

'Nothing.' I said, waving at the briefer and my butler to leave.

I remember a few weeks ago, how I was wishing for at least one respawn before I settled for life, but now that I had it, I didn't particularly feel great. I used to think that Utkarsh was enjoying his life. I feel now, that he probably turned cuckoo.

Anyway, I had to see my lady before the event. I had to tell her how much I loved her. I had to express everything that I couldn't do last time. I also had to apologize for making her think that I was like others, using her for her body. And I had to do it not because

I was afraid that I couldn't win tomorrow's competition, but because I owed it to her, I owed it to our love.

Around twenty minutes past twelve, I skedaddled from my room, in search of the princess. I knew exactly where her room was. It wasn't like I had been there before, but in the times that my lady and I were together, in all those times that she and I would lay naked beside each other, she would go on and on about how her room looked like… How she couldn't wait for me to officially enter her room… How she planned on having my baby, lots of them. I would often joke about naming our first child *Butol,* a funny and weird name, and she would always get annoyed, and we'd laugh it off, eventually falling asleep in each other's arms.

I let go off a sigh, as I found myself standing in front of a gate exactly like the princess would describe. I thought of knocking, but I didn't want to risk the guards hearing the knock. So, I softly pushed the door. To my surprise, it wasn't locked. But what was even more surprising was that the princess on seeing me didn't get emotional. In fact, she gave me a look like she didn't know who I was. This wasn't supposed to happen. I clearly remembered my mother telling me that my father tried to pursue her respawns after respawns. I didn't think of it much back then, but now as I stood there, my eyes locked with this woman who didn't even remember me, I could only imagine how romantic it would have been of my father to go after my mother even after he kept dying. People these days might call it old school stalking, but I know in my heart that it was romantic, and that's what matters. What I think of the people related to me is what matters... *what others think doesn't.*

It was weird, my lady and I staring at each other. Me admiring how beautiful she was, how much she had started glowing since the last time I had seen her, and she probably wondering who the fuck I was. But again, this wasn't supposed to happen... She wasn't supposed to forget me.

I looked down at my Heart-ball, and for some strange reason, it was glowing. Confused on what to do next, I looked around, scanning the room, when my eyes fell on this crib, and there was a baby in it.

The princess saw me staring at the baby, her expressions still not ready to acknowledge my resemblance.

'He's my child,' she continued, 'And you must be one of the suitors?'

'Yes,' I mumbled.

'You know you are not supposed to see me, don't you?'

'I... I had to. What's the name of this baby?' I asked trying to make sense of what must have gone down after I died.

'*Butol,*' she continued, 'I know it's unusual.'

And with that everything became clear. Before she

• • •

killed me, I must have made her pregnant and as a result of us now being connected in the form of our beautiful child, she now didn't remember me. It was as heartbreaking as it was beautiful, and even though I wanted to tell her everything, I didn't.

I slowly turned around preparing to leave, setting it in my mind that I was going to win the competition tomorrow. I was going to somehow get my lady and my child back, and even though they didn't have any memory of me, it was not going to stop me from making fresh memories with them.

But as I was about to step out of my lady's chamber, there was a loud thud.

In an instant, one of the guards came towards us.

'There has been an attack,' he yelled.

He then took a glance at me.

'Your Highness, I know it's not appropriate, but given the circumstances, can you please escort the princess and her baby to safety?'

We were in a situation of panic but hearing that had made me happy. I rushed towards the baby, holding him firmly in my arms, and then I helped the princess get out of her bed. The princess who was probably in a state of shock didn't say a word. She grabbed my hand without any hesitation making my Heart-ball glow brightly.

As we rushed out of the chambers, the sounds of heavy crashing and explosions followed along. Hordes of single men were running hay-wire with their Heart-balls tightly covered. It was a frightening scene because as the bombings increased, more and more men were failing at trying to save their Heart-balls from breaking and eventually vanishing into thin air.

After few minutes of trying to escape the castle, we were put to a halt, because the bombing had damaged the way ahead, and the only way to continue further was to take a steep jump.

The princess turned closer towards me, softly speaking into my ears.

'You've come for this *Swayamvar* and now you are trying to save me and my baby rather than trying to protect your Heart-ball,' she continued, 'You must truly love me?'

I don't know what it was but now that I was faced with the same question that I had failed at the last time, I wasn't going to let this moment go.

'My lady, you don't remember me,' I gushed.

She nodded.

'But I do, and apparently so does my Heart-ball.'

I continued, 'This child… He is ours. You, my lady, are mine, and, I might have not been able to say how much I loved you last time, but I am going to now.'

The princess didn't say anything. She seemed emotional but puzzled.

'I love you, and I will do my best to protect you,' I continued, 'Hold me tight my lady, because this jump

• • •

is not going to be easy, but at the end of this jump, at the end of it all, there lies a world, no Heart-ball or Cupid can comprehend.'

The princess knew she was in the right hands. She quickly wrapped her arms around me in a tight grip and with that, we jumped.

But as luck would have it, just then, another shot hit the castle blowing away where we were supposed to land, and with that, we began to fall.

The princess didn't let go of me, and I didn't let go of her and the baby, and the only way to keep them both protected from the fall was for me to take the hit first, but that would have meant that my Heart-ball would have shattered and I would have vanished. I would have lost all my memories and probably become nothing. I didn't want that. I didn't want to leave everything to fate after getting so close to my lady again. I didn't want to turn into dust.

It was only seconds before we were going to hit the ground, and my mind was constantly shuffling between all the people it had known. I thought about my mother, for some strange reason, I also thought about my neighbor's daughter; Tania, and then, my mind shuffled back to Utkarsh and what he had said once.

'*What if we destroyed it ourselves?*'

And without a second thought, I did exactly that. Moments before we were about to hit, I took a hard swing at my Heart-ball, making it shatter into pieces.

• • •

⋆La la la la, la la…⋆

'Do you know where you are?' A voice asked.

I didn't respond.

'You broke your own Heart-ball,' the voice continued.

I nodded, slowly trying to open my eyes. The tune that I would often hum was playing in the background, increasing in volume with every passing second.

⋆La la la la, la la…⋆

'And now the Heart-ball cannot respawn you back to another life,' the voice continued, 'You were destined for such great lives, do you know that?'

'Now what?' I asked, still not being able to open my eyes.

'And someone else didn't break your Heart-ball, unfortunately breaking the magical loop and preventing you from turning into dust, so…'

'So…?'

'You may now wake up.'

⋆La la la la, la la…⋆

ΔΔΔ

Samosa Party

As I stood there, in front of the entire college, I couldn't help but feel proud of myself for what I had managed to achieve. I have been going to this esteemed temple of knowledge for almost two years now, but this has literally been the defining moment of my college life. After all, I was the one to catch the notorious *Samosa* thief. Not Rahul, Not Mr. popular – Raunak, not even the security guards, but I.

And the way this college was thanking me for my efforts was no less than a surprise. The entire college premises was decorated in exotic colors, the college canteen was filled with racks and racks of *Samosas*, and at the center of it all was the new college hero; me. I swear, a day ago, I was just like any other weirdo who no one knew, but today when I was suddenly being given all the attention, I realized how great it felt to be famous in college. The college representative was a girl, a hot one for that matter, and today, since the morning, she had literally been at my beck and call, succumbing to all my stupid wishes and demands, and in return, she had only one requirement, that I support her in the upcoming elections. And I didn't mind that, after all, it wasn't like she was running for the Prime Minister, right? And even if she was, I don't think she could screw this country any more than it was already screwed.

The main event wasn't going to start for hours, and I was getting tired of posing and pouting for every female and a few males who could manage to get a chance to meet me. The last girl I took a picture with, went further ahead, bending down and posing like she was giving me a blow job. Annoyed, I signaled at the college representative, with a roll of the eyes.

'Meet me in the third-floor washroom in five minutes,' she continued, 'Now I don't mind it but you're pushing it, alright?'

At first, I was confused at what she meant by pushing it. Then, I was even more confused as to why she wanted me to meet her at a girls-only floor in a girls-only washroom. And when after a minute of thinking, I was still looking at her blankly, she began to giggle.

'Sorry, why did you call me?' she asked.

'I am hungry, can you take care of stuff over here while I go eat something,' I mumbled.

'Omg! Are you going to eat *Samosa?* Shit! This is going to be such good publicity, I am coming with you,' she cheered, instantly grabbing my hand.

You know, at that moment, a part of me really wanted to take every possible advantage of this situation, it was probably dying to chuck on the eating and actually go through with the blow job that my new hot female friend was so willing to offer, but that part of me was buried so deep into my subconscious, that the only time I was ever going to go through with something like that was going to be in my dreams.

'I am done with *Samosas* for now. I'll be eating a pizza probably,' I said, shaking her hand away.

I immediately called Utkarsh, asking him to meet me at the *Dominos* just outside our college gates.

Two hours later

'I wasn't expecting you to be calling me today,' Utkarsh said.

'Why?' I asked.

'Dude! You've been around divas since morning. I thought you'd probably be with them as long as you can.'

'What do you mean?'

'You know, how it goes?'

'Goes what?' I asked, throwing my hands up in the air.

'*Areee...*' he cried, 'All this college fandom.'

'Umm?'

'They don't last long.'

. . .

What Utkarsh had said wasn't exactly wrong. I was famous for now, but who knows, next week someone might suddenly claim he is *Shaktimaan*. And the next thing you know, all my fandom, all those selfies are being sent to the archive folder of Instagram.

'I should have gone to the third floor,' I murmured to myself.

'If we can manage to enter the college, lol,' Utkarsh chuckled, pointing his finger towards the heavily crowded gates.

I followed along the movement of his fingers, awestruck at the number of people gathered at the gates when suddenly, a group of teenagers whooshed past us and joined the crowd.

'Come, we'll enter through the swing area,' I said.

'But... Look there are so many teenagers over there,' Utkarsh said.

'So?'

'Dude! They are in line to see you, and you want to go through the other gate.'

'They can see me at the event, ok? Now let's hurry up or we'll get late.'

The swing area was like a much smaller gate, used mainly by the principal and a few old teachers. Having a few swings along its path, it led straight to the principal's office and then towards the cafeteria. And that's when we realized that using the swing entrance was a bad idea because the canteen, which is generally just a large empty room with a few students here and there, was filled to the brim. There was so much rush, that we weren't even able to stand in a single place. Hoards of fresh students were continuously pushing us from behind, and before we knew, I don't know how, but Utkarsh and I were back to where we had started from.

'How did we come out again?' I asked him, scratching my head in confusion.

He didn't respond. He just shrugged.

'Ugh! Let's just go with the crowd this time,' he then said.

'Okay,' I mumbled, 'But don't let them know that it's me.'

Utkarsh nodded and we swiftly entered through the main gates, until he pointed out something.

'Why are we walking in a curve? Aren't we supposed to walk straight?'

I tried thinking of it, but, before I could come to any conclusion, we were back, right at the start.

'Da heck! How does this keep happening to us?' I whined, in frustration.

'Are you guys trying to go inside?' Someone murmured from behind, scaring the bejesus out of us.

But, once we looked behind, we were rather shocked, than surprised. Standing behind us was someone who was definitely not from around here. He was probably from the Middle East or maybe he was Korean.

● ● ●

'Are you here to meet Doofus?' he murmured again.

Utkarsh and I stared at each other, passing a unanimous chuckle.

'Yes,' Utkarsh said.

Seeing that we were badly stuck in this situation, even I nodded.

'Are you a student in here?' I asked.

He didn't respond. The Chinese man then escorted us towards one of the entrances that stood to the right of the college. It wasn't new, in fact, the students had known about it for years now, but most of what we had known had stemmed from rumors, about how it led to some dudgeon, which led to a secret room where students of power like my earlier hot friend indulged in not so secret rendezvous.

'Excuse me? Where do you think you are going?' The security guard yelled, stopping us moments before we were about to cross the gate.

Utkarsh and I froze on our feet. We turned towards the Japanese student who was escorting us, and he was quick to respond.

'We are going to the event,' he said.

'This is a restricted gate. You cannot enter from here,' the guard said, in an affirmative voice.

Utkarsh, who was probably getting anxious about all of this tugged on my shoulder, signaling at me to do something.

'I...'

'Yes, but the event cannot happen without the celebrity, right?' the Indonesian rushed, cutting me short.

'What do you mean?'

'He is the celebrity of the event. He is Doofus.'

That was a sweet surprise. I didn't think the Burmese would recognize me, but as luck would have it, he did, and thankfully because of that, we were finally going to enter the college again.

'Oh! Hello sir,' the guard said, moving his hands forwards towards me for a shake.

I immediately shook his hand and we entered through the gate. Or, did we?

We took a flight of stairs down, at which point the Mongolian bid adieu to us. He told us that if we would continue walking up and then, take a left we should directly reach the college grounds – where the stage had been set. He also told us that Doofus was going to be at the stage any time soon and we should hurry if we wanted to catch him. For a second, I wanted to tell him about my truth, but then he asked Utkarsh if he didn't mind, him choosing the hotter person as Doofus. And between my laughing and Utkarsh's frowning, we didn't even realize that the Asian had left. Anyway, as advised, we did take a left, but we did not reach the grounds, instead, the roads led us back to where we were a few minutes earlier; the start.

At this point, both Utkarsh and I were literally clueless. How was it possible, that we were taking

● ● ●

such different roads, and yet, ending up at the very same spot. What was even more messed up was that I was the celebrity for God's sake. Why was I even going through all this ordeal? Where the fuck was my hot representative friend? Oh, god! Yes.

'The college representative,' I yelled.

'Is she here?' Utkarsh mumbled, and immediately hid beside me.

'No,' I continued, 'And why are you hiding behind me now?'

'Nothing.'

I turned around and stared straight at Utkarsh.

'I sent her a friend request a few days ago.'

'Oh! I'll call her… Wait.'

'What?' Utkarsh screamed in nervous excitement.

I didn't respond and proceeded to dial her number.

Ring Ring Ring

'Where are you?' she yelled from the phone.

'Outside the gates,' I said.

'Then, why don't you come inside?'

'Trust me, we are trying.'

'Oh shit!'

'What?'

'The education minister has put loop-holes at all the entrances of our college.'

'As in?'

'Long story short, you cannot enter the college through any of the gates.'

I paused for a second, recollecting all that had gone

through up till now. Then, I gathered all my breath and yelled:

'I am the celebrity tonight. How can I not be there?'

'Calm down Doofus!' she continued, 'Go three blocks down, and you'll find a Mosque.'

'Yes.'

'There's an entrance from there.'

'I have never been to a Mosque.'

'This is your only option right now.'

This was going to be a whole new challenge for me. People aren't wrong when they say that being a celebrity isn't an easy job, and it certainly isn't a religious one. After all, I had been famous for like ten hours, and I was already breaking my Hindu traditions by going to a Mosque.

'Listen,' I said.

'Yes?'

'I'll enter the Mosque, but…'

'Yes?'

'After the event, you and I are going to the third floor.'

'Cools, I'll bring a few of my friends along as well,' she continued, 'Now, you happy?'

'Umm… Female friends, right?'

'Yes.'

'Yay… wait?'

'Now, what?' she gushed.

'Can you bring Naina?'

'Okay,' she said and hung up.

Utkarsh, who hadn't spoken a word, all this while, started walking towards the Mosque. I quietly followed suit.

'So, how do we go inside?' I asked.

'I am not talking to you,' Utkarsh whined.

'Excuse me?'

'First, you don't tell me that you are friends with the hottest girl in our college, and now I find out that you plan on going to the third floor with her.'

'Do you want to come?'

'Yes, duh!'

'Then, let's figure out how we are going to enter the Mosque.'

'Umm?'

'Umm?'

'Yes,' Utkarsh yelled, after a minute of absolute silence.

I looked at him and smiled, waiting for him to dish out the plan.

'We both have really good beards,' he continued, 'They won't know we aren't *Muslims*.'

I remember the time when I had started keeping a beard and my mother was like: '*All this uncultured fashion isn't going to help you.*' Look, mommy! This beard is going to help me join the coveted third-floor club.

'*Doofie...* Do you like the plan?' Utkarsh questioned.

• • •

I nodded.

If you ever ask me if I take my religion seriously, I'll have one answer: I do, but only because my family does. And in my lifetime, I've been to quite a few Temples, so, I wasn't really that excited about going to a Mosque. After all, how different can it be? But then I looked at Utkarsh, and him bubbling with all the excitement, and even I was intrigued. And boy, were we surprised!

A mirror on the right, a mirror on the left. Basically, there were mirrors everywhere, except for the north side, where there was a priest, who was offering *Namaz*.

'Woah! Look at all the mirrors,' Utkarsh gushed.

'I know, I know,' I continued, 'Now let's find the gate before someone catches us.'

Utkarsh locked his eyes with mine and then with one swift motion turned towards the very large gate right in front of us.

'Look! We found it,' he said, admiring himself in one of the mirrors.

'But...'

'What?'

'Nothing.'

We swiftly entered through the gate hoping that this time, we would not get lost and actually reach where we were headed to. I know that all our other attempts had turned out to be weird, and expecting this one to be any different was a long shot, and yet I felt like this time we were going to make it. After all, this time, we were taking a leap of faith, right?

As we continued to walk along the path, the cheering of the college crowd was getting louder and louder.

We weren't there yet, but I could already hear people shouting my name repeatedly, and just when I thought that we had entered the college grounds, our journey was brought to a halt.

'What the fuck?' I yelled.

'Are those foreigners?' Utkarsh asked.

'Yes… And apparently, they are all naked.'

Utkarsh and I scanned the entire swimming pool, desperate to find some familiar face, but everywhere we looked, there was some foreigner standing naked, doing something or the other.

'Look, over there!' Utkarsh said.

'What is it?'

'He's flashing his dick at that girl,' he said and began laughing.

I turned to where Utkarsh had pointed and the foreigner was indeed doing it. Then I looked at the girl who was being flashed at.

'Naina?' I mumbled.

'Lol, yes,' Utkarsh said.

We were at a dead end now with no way to go any further, and the cheering of my name was still intact and was only growing louder. But this was not the moment to think about it. My crush… I mean my best friend's girlfriend was in danger and I had to save her. I immediately started running towards her.

'Naina…' I yelled as I continued to run.

Naina didn't respond.

'Naina…' I yelled again, immediately signaling at the foreigner to leave her alone.

'Open your eyes,' Naina gushed, splashing the swimming pool's water on my face.

'Are you safe?' I continued, 'Where am I?'

'The third floor,' Naina said.

'Already? Is the event over? Where's the college representative?'

Naina looked at me and facepalmed. She then began laughing.

'Why are you laughing?' I asked, puzzled.

'You don't remember, do you?'

'What?'

'You bumped into the college rep, splashed a *chutney* filled *Samosa* on her, and then, you fainted.'

ΔΔΔ

The Cyclone Escape

It's been a week since we have been here. A five-year-old kid, his two-year-old sister, and their proud parents, all stranded in the Tsunami that shook the Andaman Islands a week ago and has, since, been raging on.

I have no idea which one of my parents had this idea of going on an unplanned vacation because vacations are supposed to make you happy, but after two weeks of being locked into this place, I am still happy. After all, I was only five and these natural disasters had not yet formed a part of my limited knowledge, and I had absolutely no clue that Tsunamis were supposed to be scary.

'It's all part of a game,' my father continued, 'You kids are having fun, right?'

I looked at my father with surprise, I then looked at my sister, who was crying because she was hungry, I then lent an ear towards the mess radio that kept speaking of words like *horror* and *death*. Finally, I hopped towards my mother.

It has been eight days since my entire family and around a hundred others have been stranded in the hall of *Hotel Andaman Residency*; A five-star hotel, once famous for its glorious beach view. Well, now? Not so much. All that remained now was this hall and its hundred survivors, eagerly waiting for the rescue team to come and take everyone away.

Hummmmmmmmmmm

'The plane's here,' someone from the crowd in the room yelled.

And a bunch of adults rushed out, swimming their way towards the sound coming from the open skies. After all, the food was here. I had been taught that food was grown by farmers, but this was a strange place because, here, packets of food would drop straight from the sky – I wanted to find out who exactly was dropping them. For the first few days, I even thought that farmers lived in the sky. I asked my father about it and after he told me the truth, I started pitying my school teacher for the mirage that she was living in.

Moments later, my father returned inside with a pamphlet in his hand. He looked happy, which was quite ironic because everyone around him looked sad. He quickly gathered everyone around him into a circle and started reading from the pamphlet while the others who had gone out with him distributed the limited food to us.

'The Government and the Army are trying their level best, but due to the early arrival of the cyclone, major rescue operations have been stopped and only a few rescue boats will be sent out before the cyclone hits the islands,' my father read out loud.

The entire crowd, which was busy grabbing the food, suddenly broke out in unison. Amidst all the murmurs, swear words like *'Screw the Government'* kept recurring. My mother walked towards me and cuddled me in her arms. She held my sister's hand and suddenly, started crying.

'Bhagwan hamare sath hai... hame kuch ho hi nai sakta,' she said, as a drop of tear rolled down her cheek and fell on my shoulder. (God is with us... Nothing bad can happen to us.)

'Why is dad happy?' I asked her.

She didn't reply.

The mess hall that had been our shelter for the week was a very big hall. Beautiful paintings hung out on its walls, the windows were draped in royal curtains, and there was a large chandelier in the center, adding to its grand architecture, that is, until the disaster struck. It had four doors, each leading to a part of the hotel, and a staircase leading towards the mighty water. Of this beautiful and marvelous structure, now only the staircase remained, and oh yes! The water.

Around three hours later, a loud revving sound

came from outside, along with the usual thundering and all the people started to cheer and so did I, though unsure of the reason.

For the first time, my father let me out to the staircase, along with him and the other men in the hall, to graciously welcome the revving sound, while the mothers and grandmothers in the crowd started thanking the Almighty. The cheers were growing louder and the men started to howl like beasts as the revving continued, and so did the cyclone at the distant sea, *but that seemed like past news to them.*

I remember, once my friend in school had told me about this word called *'mood swings'* and how we humans keep having it from time to time, I didn't quite understand it back then, but now I had a clear idea because what looked like a bunch of wolves celebrating their successful hunting just a while ago, were now looking like a group of mourners who had just lost a common aunt. Nonetheless, the revving made me feel excited, as I counted the number of boats from one up to ten and stared at the two men standing inside each one of them.

The men looked at each other with blank eyes, each one of their faces depicting a different emotion. I looked at one of them and he looked sad, the one at the corner look terrified, the other had his fingers crossed. Deeply upset by what I was seeing, I turned towards my father and unlike others he still was calm… He patted on my head and whispered 'Never

• • •

lose hope… *beta,* for hope, is all that we have. Without hope, we are already dead, for then, there is no purpose left to live.'

My father's words struck my heart like a bolt and I felt as if something very bad was going to happen, something that might change the course of my future. A future that was so close, I could hear it right through the sounds of thunder and the abundance of rain, preparing itself to strike.

The boats were drawing closer and closer by the seconds as the murmurs amongst the men continued.

'This is bull shit,' someone yelled.

'How will we all fit inside?' another one exclaimed.

'The government will have to pay for this.'

I could see a few people counting something in their fingers. Excited, even I began counting, but after three long minutes of practicing math, I was confused… as the boats were not enough to accommodate even half of us. This meant that the societal customs would triumph over moral judgment, and the first to be rescued would be the kids and the elderly. Even the thought of this made me bite my lips because this meant that I would be on one of these boats soon while my parents would have to wait in queue for a chance at survival.

The rescue men approached us with a ton of confidence, but a tensed look, because they knew that soon most of us would be dead and there was nothing, they could do but act – act with hope. They explained to us that each of their boats could carry five more people and the safety location was another hour from here, but they promised that they would return for the rest of them again and instead of reacting, we needed to act because time and luck, both had sided with the devil and the devil could strike anytime soon.

The murmurs now turned into anger, anger into a rage, and rage brought chaos, but the rescue men did their best to control the situation. They led us back to the hall, where people still were hopeful, in unanimous prayers, completely unaware of the number of boats that had arrived outside. The men had neither the words nor the courage to explain their plight so they kept numb and their silence did have the desired effect. All the women broke out, expressing their fears through tears in their eyes.

Even the rescue people kept staring at us for a while, but they had to act fast, because they had to return again, to fulfill the promise that they had made. They quickly took charge, dividing us into groups of children, the elderly and the adults. Each child was to be accompanied by one parent and those who would be left by would have to wait for the boats to return.

There were twenty children including me and my sister and eighteen elderlies. This meant that not all the kids would be having a parent by his side and that was not a good thing. Each one out there was coming up with different kinds of reasoning and logic, of which most of them explained why they had to be on the boat before anyone else, but the rescue people did not pay any heed and urged them to stay calm and follow the rules. Some elders, being wise, offered to stay, and even I agreed to that. After all, they didn't have much to live for anyway, right?

All this while I had been standing beside my mother who held my hand tight while my sister clung to mother's saree on the other side. Her hands were trembling with fear as she gazed hopelessly towards my father who could do nothing but smile at us.

'*Agar mujhe aur tere papa ko kuch ho jaye, toh apni behen ka hamesha khayal rakhna, promise kar mujhe Doofus,*' she said, looking deep into my eyes, conveying all her motherly emotions, for words could not express what her eyes could. I looked at my mother, then at my sister and bit my lips hard. I had nothing to say. (Promise me that you will take care of your sister if anything happens to your father and I.)

All children were now being provided with life jackets but the real problem remained. Rounds of arguments followed but a mutual understanding could not be achieved. With little time in hand and continuing chaos, my father eventually stepped forward to be amongst the ones to stay back and that sparked a movement as a few others followed him and the rescue operation finally started. My mother kept staring emotionlessly at my father who could do nothing, but smile.

My father came to us and hugged us all, he spoke

something to my mother which I could not hear and then, he waved at us with a smile. The rescue men kept explaining various rules and drills while we were being escorted to the boats. My mother kept staring at the mess hall, still without emotions, as we continued to move ahead and sat on those boats. The rescue men wasted no further time and sailed the boats away while those left out there waved at us, some crying, some smiling and some just looking down into the abyss of their agony.

"Due to heavy rain-fall, today's fire drill is canceled. I repeat, due to heavy rainfall, today's fire drill is canceled, over," the school secretary announced, over the public address system.

ΔΔΔ

Author's Note: This was the very first dream that I had consciously accepted, and when I woke up, I was like – Dude! What was this? I wrote this story years ago when I was in class twelve. Who would have thought back then, that this dream of mine would someday turn into a book!

Stand-Up Comedy

I let go of a sigh. A bit nervous, but more excited, I, then, gripped the mic steadily in my hands, and bringing it closer to my lips, I began to speak:

'So, I've been wondering lately,' I continued, 'There are all kinds of animals, right? And all these animals have different kinds of sounds.'

I paused for a second, waiting for the audience to create a sort of a vague mental image of random animals roaming freely in their minds. Then I continued.

'And a few of them are also kept as pets... So, basically, a *Cat* that *Meows* goes by the name *Lucifurr*.'

There was a soft chuckle amongst the audience.

'God! Why even call it Cat? Why just not call it Meow? I'll yell from my room "*Meow*", Meow will yell from a spooky part of the house, *"Meow"*, and we'll both get on with our lives,' I continued, 'Maybe that's why cats are such bitches, they want you to call them *Meow*. Not *Lucifurr*, not *Mr. Cat*, just *Meow*.'

The entire audience meowed in laughter.

Happy that the opening joke of my first ever *half-pant stand-up open-mic* had done so well, I scanned the room in excitement until my eyes stuck on this one girl who looked a tad too familiar. But before I could deal with the task of moving on to the next joke, while also figuring out who the person was, she was greeted by another familiar *Hooman*. Only this one, I knew a bit too well.

Why was she here? Why is it that whenever something important happens in my life, she somehow becomes a part of it? Is the universe in its own twisted way trying to tell me that she, in fact, is the one?

By now, I had been lost in my thoughts for so long, that the entire room had turned silent. They were probably waiting for my next punchline, they were probably silently laughing at my inability to continue, or maybe, I was making this all up in my head. I continued:

'This girl, she tells me,
she is now ready, to look
for love. A dozen poetries,
her friends getting married,
have unanimously convinced
her, that it's finally time, she
lived off, another crappy human.
A feminist at heart, but a romantic
at soul, she then recalls all those
pesky childhood stories. So, with
a shoe in her hand, and optimism
in her bones, she sets out in her
search, for a prince, worthy of all
her glory. In cafes, in meadows,
she looks, even in malls. Aghast,
she then asks me: Where is a
man, who'll keep me warm, all
through winter...?'

And suddenly, it hit me. No, not a thought, but a big, red, and juicy tomato… straight at my chest.

A guy got up from his seat, gave me a weird look and yelled, 'This is a comedy open-mic, go recite your poem at your school.'

Then another guy hurled another tomato at me, this time hitting me on my hand, causing the mic to drop. That's when I realized that in all this multi-tasking, my single-core mind had managed to make a fool of me. But I wasn't going to let this happen, not

• • •

in front of Rhea at least. I remember we were taught in school, that two negatives make a positive. So, I, Doofus, calmed my stupid brain, reached for the mic, and as I slowly began to stand back up, I continued:

'I stare at her,
then I chuckle. Oh, girl! Don't
you know? Soulmates are
now found on Tinder?'

And just like that, my first ever *Half-pant stand-up open-mic* became a success. Not only was I given a standing ovation in the end, but a few of the ladies also tossed their numbers at me. And all of this happening in Rhea's presence was the perfect icing on the cake.

Once my performance was over, Rhea suddenly started walking towards me, making my heart beat very fast. I don't know why, but for some strange reason, I thought that she was coming to hug me. And why not? After all, we were seeing each other after such a long time. A year to be exact.

So, I opened my arms wide, eagerly waiting for her to embrace my body, but just like that, she simply walked past me, stopping in front of the emcee.

For a moment, I thought, that I was going to have to live with this embarrassment for my entire life, but then Rhea's sister quickly walked up to the stage, and gracefully completed my hug.

'Your jokes were so lame,' She continued, 'I couldn't stop myself from laughing.'

'Thank you...' I mumbled.

• • •

'It's good to see you, *Doofie*... How have you been?'

'Great, I guess.'

Even though Rhea's sister had saved me from the embarrassment, I couldn't help but think about the fact that Rhea had simply ignored my presence. We were off the stage by now, and between our casual chit-chatting, I was taking every chance I could get to glance at Rhea. And, Rhea's sister obviously noticed it.

'The emcee's her boyfriend,' she said.

I swear, hearing that had made me very uneasy, but I wasn't going to let my uneasiness show.

'That's okay,' I blurted, 'But, she could have at least greeted me, right?'

'Yes, but...'

'Umm?'

'How do I even say this,' Rhea's sister mumbled.

'Say what?'

'That she has no memory left of you.'

'WHAAAT?' I yelled, making the entire audience turn their heads towards us.

But, when I didn't speak anything for like a minute, they were back to what they do best; staring at their phones, while some random person performs on the stage.

'So, you're saying that she doesn't remember who I am?' I asked.

'Nope,' Rhea's sister said.

'Nothing at all? Does she even remember Fuck-boy?'

'No, and... No.'

'But... Why... How?'

'Who's this friend of yours? Aren't you going to introduce him to me?' Rhea said, cutting our conversation short.

I glanced at Rhea, and she looked beautiful as always. Then I noticed Rhea's emcee boyfriend who had his arms wrapped around Rhea's waist and I couldn't bear it. So, I softly held Rhea's hand as one would greet someone, planted a kiss on the backside of her palm, and in one swift motion, pulled her closer towards the empty chair between Rhea's sister and I. Rhea, who couldn't have possibly gauged what I had done, gladly sat on the chair, hence completing my master plan. Rhea's sister who was obviously noticing everything, couldn't help herself from laughing, and only after I rolled her eyes at her, did she stop.

'I am Doofus,' I continued, 'And you must be Rhea?'

'Well, yes. I am... Nice to meet you, Doofus.'

Rhea then turned towards her sister.

'He's quite a charmer. Why haven't you told me about him before?' She teased.

Rhea's sister didn't respond. She probably wasn't expecting that something like this would happen.

'Well, she wanted to introduce me in person.' I said to break the silence.

• • •

'I really liked your performance,' Rhea's sister said.

Ahem Ahem The emcee coughed and then tugged on Rhea's shoulders.

'Hey man! Don't you have to introduce the next performer?' I said, looking right at him.

He didn't respond, and I knew quite well that his silence was that of jealousy, but he did have to get back to the stage. He came closer to us, looked at me, and smiled. Then, he turned towards Rhea and kissed on her cheek. He then looked back at me, smiled again and finally went back to the stage.

'Nice boyfriend you have there,' I said.

Rhea took out a napkin and wiped her cheek where the emcee had kissed.

'He's alright,' she said.

This was weird. First, the wiping, and then her snide remark – Those weren't exactly the signs of a happy woman. And they certainly weren't indicative of a woman in love. Was she not happy? Wait, how did she not remember me in the first place?

'Are you going to perform today?' I asked Rhea.

'Lol! Me? Comedy? *Nooo,*' she gushed.

Unfortunately, for us, that was the last that we talked for the entire event. It wasn't like I didn't want to, but I still didn't know what had happened to her, and she didn't initiate a conversation either. Yes, there were a few chuckles once in a while, but that was mainly because of the *half-pant stand-up open-mic* that we were a part of.

. . .

'*And now, after a gap of one whole year, I am going to perform on stage,*' the emcee said at the end of the event.

And everyone started clapping. Everyone, but Rhea.

I noticed this and asked her, 'You don't like comedy much, do you?'

'Oh! I do. I really liked yours… Why?' she said.

'Umm… Nothing.'

Something was surely very fishy, and luckily, I didn't have to wait much to find out. For once Rhea's beloved emcee started performing, it was clear why Rhea wasn't exactly happy about today.

Now, I am not sure what his jokes exactly were, but most of them were about his girlfriend and the crazy stupid things that she did. And, even though he wasn't using Rhea's name, it was pretty obvious – it was her. With every new joke, the laughter of the audience would increase and so would the uneasiness of Rhea.

'Hey *Doofie*, would you like to go for a walk with me?' Rhea suddenly asked.

This had caught me by surprise. I looked at Rhea's sister, who nodded in approval, and then, Rhea and I got up and left the hall. I don't know what the emcee's reaction was since we didn't look back, but the fact that he took a pause as soon as we got up was enough to know that he didn't like what he saw.

The *half-pant stand-up open-mic* was taking place in a very unique place. It was a hotel, but unlike other hotels, this one was by the river. No, not just by the river, in fact, it was on the river. It wasn't floating or anything, but it wasn't still either. The waves, if strong enough were sure to affect a seasick person, and the fact that there was water on three sides only added to the experience.

So, Rhea and I were walking along the riverbank amidst a strange sort of silence. It wasn't romantic, but it wasn't awkward either. There was a certain kind of vibe to us, and I am sure that Rhea, despite her loss of memory, could sense it. It was a chilly night, and being on the riverbank, with the wind blowing right at us was only making it chillier. So, what Rhea did next might be breaking stereotypes, but I really needed it.

'You must be freezing in that half pant,' Rhea said.

I looked down on the cemented passage, my hands inside my pocket, and started walking in a twisted sort of way.

'Maybe,' I mumbled.

Rhea immediately took off her jacket, and instead of giving it to me, she began to tie it around my waist. I swear, as her hands touched my back, I could literally feel my heart skip a beat.

'You didn't have to do that,' I gushed.

Rhea completed the tying and then began walking again. For a few seconds, I just stood there, engrossing myself in the beauty of what had just happened, and it was only after Rhea signaled at me, that I did begin walking again, quickly catching on to her.

'You don't remember me, do you?' I eventually asked her.

'Umm… Were you at my sister's birthday party?' she asked, a bit puzzled.

'No,' I continued, 'But I was at yours.'

'You were?'

Rhea stopped walking, turning her face towards me.

'Were you and I close?' she asked.

I didn't respond.

'The thing is,' she continued, 'A few months ago, I got heavily drunk…'

'Shit! And?'

'And I was driving, and I remember driving to this then sort-of boyfriend of mine or so my sister tells me.'

Hearing that made my eyes instantly light up.

'Anyway, on my way back, I met with an accident,' she continued, 'And I woke up in a hospital a few weeks later with no memory of what happened to me in the past two years.'

I heard Rhea's story patiently, but from the moment she mentioned that she got drunk and went to see this sort of boyfriend of hers, I knew something was not right. You see, when your mind deals with various levels of craziness on a daily basis, no matter how stupid you are, on some level you tend to grasp what's real and what's not. At that moment, I instantly

• • •

knew that all of this was happening inside of my head, and my brain in its desperate attempt was trying to hold onto something emotional in any way it could. It was probably trying to give me a happy ending so that when I woke up, I would actually be happy rather than the pretending which I always do.

'Rhea!' I cried, 'You never came to my house.'

Rhea looked at me with googly eyes.

'I didn't?' she asked.

'Nope... And you didn't meet with any accident.'

'I didn't?'

'Nope... And if it wasn't for Fuck-boy, you would have always loved me.'

'I loved you?'

'Nope?'

ΔΔΔ

The Plates

Essssssssssss

I was numbly staring at the water filter, while I hopelessly waited for the jug to fill. In a desperate attempt to amuse myself, I started moving the jug up and down, making the sound of the water go from a heavy pitch to a lighter one.

Esssssuuuuuuussssse

As the dripping water continued to fill the jug, my mind filled itself with the memories of everything that had gone wrong, the last time I had come to this place.

'I couldn't save this world last time, but I will save it now,' I repeated in my head.

Once the jug filled, I placed it on the hotel room's side-table and tucked myself inside the cozy blanket. I had come to this place years ago, and even back then, I had stayed in this very room. Nothing has changed since then. That water filter, the wooden side-table, the CRT television, even the blue stain on my cozy blanket, everything's exactly the same as it used to be. Now, I know that the bluish stain was totally my doing, but, the fact that it was still present only made forgetting my last time's failed attempt harder.

I looked at the wall clock just in front of me, as the minute's hand inched closer to ten, but my staring was interrupted by a buzz on my phone.

Ring Ring Ring

It was a video call from my Guru.

'Namaste Guruji,' I said, picking up the call.

Guruji raised his hand to give me his blessings.

'I've found the location of the tenth plate,' he said, in a calm and composed voice.

And in an instant, my eyes lit up.

I got up from my bed and quickly reached for my bag, which was lying beside the side-table. I took out a huge map that was folded in half, and after placing the map flat open on the bed, I turned back towards my Guru.

'So, where is it?' I asked.

Guruji, who was the audience to my activities all this while, closed his eyes. He asked me to place the tip of my finger on any point on the map and slowly move it in a random manner.

I thought for a second, eventually deciding to start with the rightmost corner, where I had found my first plate. I placed my finger on *Revada* – An island like no other. *Revada* wasn't that big. Sure, it was an island kingdom, but the king's castle was the only thing that was there on the island, and even that was so fragile, that it hung by a rope. I sighed, recalling how my previous attempt had almost wrecked *Revada's* fragile castle.

By this time, my random movements had brought my finger to almost the center of the map, and just when I was about to cross the location of my hotel, *Guruji* said stop.

All this while, I had my phone positioned in such a way that *Guruji* could clearly see the map, and I, at the same time could see what *Guruji* was doing. So, I knew for sure that he hadn't opened his eyes until he had asked me to stop.

'Where is this place?' he asked me.

I remained silent for a second, and then, instead of telling him, I simply switched to the back camera of my phone.

'So, it's here?' he then asked.

'Yes,' I said.

'You have the other plates with you?'

I switched back to the front camera and nodded.

'I'll call you in the morning, you take rest now,' he said, and hung up.

Wait, what? After telling me that the final plate was right here in this place, how could *Guruji* simply ask me to take rest? But then, *Guruji* always had a purpose behind whatever he said, so, I obliged and went back to bed.

• • •

For almost thirty minutes, I just laid there, while my mind hung onto the new revelation. And when it was fairly certain that I wasn't going to fall asleep with all that anxiousness building up inside me, I thought to take a trip down the memory lane.

I remembered how after I had gotten the first plate from *Revada*, I had to indulge in a verbal fight with the guards just so I could leave. I also remembered how my fifth plate had sort of come to me as a gift from winning a lottery at the carnival. I also remembered how one of the plates was given to me by a Guru just like my *Guruji*. 'Your dreams will get fulfilled one day,' he had said to me.

But dreams don't get fulfilled if you don't work on them, do they? I sprung up from the bed and reached for my bag.

I placed the green plate to my left, it had strange branchy patterns that looked like a dried leaf. I then took out the plate which had a cow engraved on it, that I had received from the only farmer in the land, and placed it beside the green one. Next, I closed my eyes and took out a random plate. This one was the one with two Suns. I placed this one beside the cow. I peeked into my bag, and there were five more plates, of which, four were exactly the same. So, I took out the odd one out which had the energy symbol on it.

'So, there is a leaf, a cow, an energy symbol, two Suns, and five waters,' I murmured to myself, just when my phone buzzed.

* * *

'Couldn't sleep?' *Guruji* asked as soon as I picked up the call.

'How did you know?' I continued, 'Ugh! Who am I asking! You're *Guruji*... You know everything.'

Guruji let go of a chuckle. 'Your phone's mic is connected to our servers,' he said.

'And it's on... *All... The time?*' I stammered.

Guruji didn't respond. It looked like he was doing some sort of calculation in his head with his eyes dead fixated on the plates.

After around a minute of staring, he turned towards me and said, 'Take out the water plates.'

I took them out and placed them beside the energy plate, stacking them on top of each other.

'We already know that the plates are connected,' *Guruji* said.

I nodded.

'And now we know that the last plate is here.'

I nodded again.

'Take all the water plates and place them on the floor.'

I did as *Guruji* had said and then returned back to the call.

'Now place your hand on the green plate and close your eyes while I chant the holy mantra.'

Guruji began to mumble something, and around a minute later, he asked me to open my eyes.

'Now place this plate over the first water plate,' he said.

• • •

I swear, I have no idea about the kind of magic my *Guruji* is capable of, but now that he had chanted the mantra, the plate seemed heavier than before. And not just by a margin, in fact, it had gotten so heavy that I couldn't lift it with one hand. So, I placed the phone aside, and then, picked up the plate to place it over the water plate on the floor.

And as soon as I did it, the green plate began to glow. Various shades of green were now emitting from the four sides of the plate, and forming a curve, eventually meeting at a point a few meters above and then vanishing into oblivion.

I immediately picked my phone up so that even *Guruji* could see what was happening and as we continued to ogle at the visual delight, lines started to emerge from the branchy engraving on the plate and took the shape of a leaf.

'You get it?' *Guruji* asked.

I nodded, and quickly placed my hand on the cow plate.

'Let's do the next one,' I exclaimed.

Guruji and I went through the exact same steps, and after we were done, we now had a plate with not one, but two cows. After this, we proceeded with the plate with two Suns, but to our surprise, nothing happened this time.

We thought for a while as to what must have gone wrong and as always, *Guruji* eventually came up with a solution.

• • •

'The Sun doesn't need water,' he said.

'Yes,' I said.

'But water evaporates in the Sun.'

'So, we switch the plates?' I asked.

Guruji nodded.

I immediately switched the plates and in an instant the water symbol from the plate vanished. I thought I'll proceed with the energy plate now, but something was amiss. All the other plates had stopped glowing after their engravings had changed, but this one was still glowing brightly in a yellow and reddish hue. This time, I didn't need to turn to *Guruji* for an answer, because I already knew the solution. I took another water plate and placed it on top of the existing one. The water engraving instantly vanished and so did the bright glow.

We were now left with an energy plate and a water plate, and as far as I could understand, like last time, the water plate was supposed to go on top of the energy one, and so it did. Within moments, the entire process was done, but the water, instead of vanishing, turned into the shape of ice.

'So far so good,' I continued, 'But what do we do now?'

'I had my doubts,' *Guruji* said.

'About?'

'And after the map incident...'

Guruji was about to finish his sentence when suddenly, the leaf plate began to glow again. It glowed for a while, and then the glowing began to fade. Moments later, the engraving on the plate started to crumble.

'What do we do now? I asked *Guruji*.

'We need water to save the leaves,' he said.

'But we don't have any more left,' I said.

'Hmm.'

'Can't we use ice?'

Guruji thought for a second and then advised me to use the Sun, but as soon as I tried bringing the Sun closer to the leaf, it started emitting a burning glow and heat began to come out of it.

'There's no saving the leaf now,' I continued, 'Better we just use it.'

'You're right, Doofus!' *Guruji* said.

'I am?'

'Feed the leaves to the cows... I mean, place the green plate over the cow.'

I did so and then *Guruji* began to explain again how he was almost certain that he knew what the last plate was, but before he could reveal it to me, another incident happened.

The ice on the water plate that was above the energy plate sort of began to melt, and at the same time water started to emerge inside the cow plate.

'Look at this!' I exclaimed.

'Do you know why the leaves were drying?' *Guruji* asked.

'Because we were short of water?'

'No! We had water… Look at the plates… We still have a lot of it.'

'Then?'

'We didn't have usable water.'

I nodded.

'Do you know why the Sun wasn't useful?' *Guruji* asked again.

'No, I don't.'

'Because it's become too harsh for the leaf.'

'How so?'

'You can see the ice melting, right?'

'Yes.'

'And where is it going?'

'To the cows.'

'Yes.'

'And what will happen once all the ice melts?'

'The cows will drink it,' I said in a proud and exciting tone.

'No, *Doofie*! Rem? This water isn't of any use…'

'Oh! Yes. Then?'

'The cows will drown.'

I looked at the plates as the water continued to melt, increasing by the second.

'What if we find the last plate? It might solve all the problems,' I continued, 'You said, you know what the last plate is?'

Guruji looked at me and sighed heavily.

'I do, but…' he said.

'But?'

'The last plate isn't the cure. It's the cause of it all.'

As the words came out of *Guruji*'s mouth, my eyes were caught wide in surprise. Meanwhile, all the ice had melted, and the cows after drowning, had vanished. Not sure what to do, I placed the now empty ice plate on top of the Sun plate followed by the empty cow plate.

'What is the last plate?' I asked *Guruji*.

'It's me.'

'You?' I asked, surprised.

'It's also you… It's all of us.'

'Us humans are the last plate? Us humans are the cause of it…'

Before I could finish my sentence, all the nine plates which now stood in a single file began to glow. There was a loud crackling sound followed by a sudden flash. The flash was then followed by complete darkness with only the plates glowing. Nothing else was visible, not even the phone which I had in my hand all this while. And it wasn't that I might have dropped the phone because I could still feel its weight on my palm.

Suddenly, there was a humming sound coming from the plates, and once the humming stopped, a mysterious voice spoke.

'Welcome monster,' it said.

'I am Human,' I mumbled.

'Are you?'

'Who are you?'

'I am Earth.'

'Our Earth?'

'You don't destroy something if you consider it yours,' it said.

'But...'

'You don't misuse something that you consider yours.'

'But...'

'You're not supposed to hurt the very thing that keeps you alive.'

'But...'

'What?'

'Who are you, again?'

The voice didn't respond for some time and just when I thought I had lost it, the tenth plate emerged from the glow. It had a human figure engraved on it. The floating plate came and rested on my palm where I had my phone.

'You are the tenth plate, and what you choose next will decide my fate,' the voice said.

'Listen, Mr. Earth! First of all, my name is Doofus, not that you care,' I continued, 'And you talk about us misusing this Earth... You say that we are destroying the limited resources that we have, right?'

'Yes,' it replied.

'Then why didn't you emerge when I tried to save you five years ago?' I continued, 'Why did you not give me a chance back then?'

'You weren't ready,'

'For?'

'In a few seconds, three doors shall emerge in front of you.'

'Okay.'

'The first one is your past, the second one is your present, and the third is your future.'

'And I have to pick one?'

'I shall give you the power to turn my limited resources to as much as you want, and the *as much part* shall amplify the further ahead you go in time.'

'And what will happen to the time that I leave behind?'

'That shall be wiped off.'

'You mean like a trade-off?'

'Yes.'

'Can I talk to *Guruji*?'

'No.'

'Can you suggest me something?'

'No.'

'Can I at least talk to the hotel manager? I need to pay the bill.'

'What, no!'

'You're mean, you know that?'

'And you aren't?'

'Earth! I am not mean. I am Doofus.'

'Make a choice!'

All this time, while I was making stupid conversations with the Earth, my mind was making calculations of its own.

• • •

If I went to the future, I might make the Earth survive for the longest, but that would also wipe out all living beings that have existed or might exist before the point I chose and without the very existence of memories, whose cause was I even serving? The purpose of all of this is supposed to be to save and prolong humanity. We need to save our Earth, not for the sake of Earth, but for the sake of us and our generations to come. So, going to the future would have been in its very essence going back to the start, and that wasn't the kind of future I was interested in.

I then thought about the past, I thought about going to a point when all of the exploitation might have begun. Yes, I might be going with the least amount of resources, but if I could curb the issue in its ground, I could have created a better future, right? But then I realized that this would have been a major mistake for two big reasons. First of all, me going to a bunch of curious and greedy men, with more resources than they already had, wasn't going to help the cause. It would make them more careless and that would have been counter-productive. Secondly, as science says, we cannot change the future by changing our past – We can only create an alternate future. So, going to the past was also not an option.

So, at the heart of it all, my only choice was to go back to the present – My present, and showcase the perfectly balanced gain of new resources as a sort of technological improvement and then try and rationalize the thought of not just our Earth, but us also dying into the minds of each and every human. Moreover, the younger generation of my present was already more nature cautious than those of the past. And being in the present and trying a bit harder to re-shape the future seemed like the most obvious choice.

The voice from the plates, which was still glowing brightly, hadn't spoken for so long. I was ready to convey my decision, but before I could, I noticed something unusual.

'Hey, Earth?' I muttered.

'Yes?'

'Why do I feel like I am wet?'

'*Haye Ram! Fir moot diya yeh larka... College me aa gaya lekin abhi bhi bistar mein susu karne ki aadat nahi gayi iski,*' the voice yelled. (Oh God! He's wet the bed again. Who's going to believe that he's in college, huh!)

ΔΔΔ

Coma Story

T he best thing about having a family is, simply, having a family. It's both, good and bad, and the bad and the good complement each other in such a way, that it makes up for all the emotions in the world. Because at the heart of it all, these are the people God chose for you, and God cannot be wrong, can he?

Sure, there can be a few characters who just don't add up. Sure, there can be people who even though are bound to you by blood, still, hate the very presence of you. And sure, if God deliberately chose you to be stuck with such people, maybe he believes that, even though they are bad, you have a heart pure enough to make them good.

My life was no exception. I lived in a joint family, with my father, my mother, two of my cousins and the cousin's parents, and just like I mentioned earlier, the person, whose heart I was supposed to mend, was my mother.

It was a week before my exams, and I was more than prepared for it. My mother, who also used to teach me at home, couldn't have been prouder by the progress I had been making, but none of those happy emotions could ever make their way out of her stubborn ego. It had been slightly less than an hour, and we still had around fifteen minutes to go in our daily study schedule, but with no study left to do, I thought, I'll use this opportunity to try and bond with my mother.

I was going to tell my mother something very special. And in spite of the fact, that it was completely unrelated to what we generally talked about, I really wanted my mother to be the first one to know. After all, I knew it in my heart that of all the people, she was going to be the person who would not only understand but also guide me in the best possible way.

'Mom,' I said, 'Did you hear about what happened to Naina?'

My mother looked at me and sighed.

'Rahul's friend? Aren't they in a relationship?' she asked.

'Yes… I mean No. They broke up a week ago.'

'Oh! Poor fellow. Naina was a good girl.'

'Yes!'

I paused for a moment and then continued again.

'I am in love with Naina,' I mumbled.

I was hoping that after all the stories I had heard of

my mother going against all odds, to marry the man of her dreams, of standing up against her family, her rituals, she'll know that even though wrong, my feelings were innocent. I was hoping that for once, she won't lash out at me as she does on a daily basis, and actually give me some advice.

Rather, she stood up, looked dead at my eye, and soon began her non-stop high-pitched rambling of how big a disgrace I was to the family. She kept calling out on my actions, and even though, I wanted to apologize to her, I just didn't know what wrong had I done. Her rambling went on and on for as long as I could remember, maybe longer than it usually did. And in the end, when she threatened to kill herself if I didn't give up on this crappy idea of love, I just couldn't take it anymore. My entire body froze, and within seconds, I fell down on the spot.

My cousin tells me that it was he, who found me lying on the ground and immediately took me to the hospital. My mother who stood there motionless accompanied him and never left the hospital till I came back home, which was a whole week later.

The doctors had advised me complete bed rest for another month, and since the atmosphere at my home wasn't particularly great, my friends would often come and visit me to make sure that I was doing fine. The whole lot of them – even Naina.

'So, you slept for seven whole days!' Utkarsh gushed.

• • •

I didn't say anything.

'And the doctor now wants him to sleep for a month more,' Rahul added.

And both of them started laughing.

Just then, my mother walked into the room, and normally my stupid friends are *Sanskari* enough to take her blessings by touching her feet, but things were different now. No one was talking to her since I went into coma, not even them.

My mother scanned the entire room and it wasn't difficult for her to find what she was looking for, after all, Naina was the only girl present. She walked up to her and smiled, and she left, without saying a word.

My friends continued to visit me at every chance they could get, but things had been very awkward between Naina and Rahul since their break-up and that awkwardness was always visible. So, a week later, Rahul suddenly laughed off that I was completely fine and he wasn't going to visit me anymore. It was only Utkarsh and Naina left now, but Utkarsh lived a bit too far, and traveling all the way to my home wasn't easy for him, so after another week, it was just Naina visiting me, and even though I was more than happy to spend some time alone with her, I couldn't help but think about all the events that had led up to this, and how she, unknowingly was the reason that I was in this mess.

Naina and I would talk for hours alone, and from visiting every alternate day, she would now come to see me every single day, and we'd just sit and talk, or watch her favorite movie. I had often tried asking her why she and Rahul broke up, but she would always change the topic to something completely unrelated.

All was going fine. Even my mother, whom I thought would be cynical with the fact that Naina and I were spending so much time alone, didn't react about it. She'd come to my room every now and then, smile at us, and then leave without saying anything. Then there was our family doctor, who'd visit every four days to check up on me, and would always make it a point to credit Naina for my speedy recovery, making her bubble with joy. As I said, everything was fine, until, Rahul, who wouldn't dare call me in the evenings, called me.

'Hey, *Doofie!* Naina's there?' he asked.

'Yup,' I said.

'Put the call on the speaker then,' he said.

Naina looked at me curiously, and as soon as she realized that the call was from Rahul, she bit her tongue. She was sitting on the chair, while I was tucked in my bed. She immediately paused the movie that was playing on the laptop and hopped on to the bed, sitting right beside me.

'Hey,' she mumbled, facing the phone.

'Have you told him why we broke-up?' Rahul asked.

I turned towards Naina, looking at her wide-eyed.

'No,' she said.

'Umm… Why did you break up?' I asked.

'Naina!' Rahul exclaimed.

'*Aye.*'

'She's in love with someone else,' Rahul said.

Hearing those words had caught me by surprise. I couldn't have imagined that there was someone else in her life, and to be honest, after spending so much time with her, my feelings for her had only gotten stronger. I thought that Naina was now going to tell us about her so-called boyfriend, but instead, she had covered her face with her hands, as if she was blushing.

'And from the way I see you look at her, I know that you like her as well,' Rahul continued.

Did I just hear that? Naina, who had been covering her face, removed her hands and smiled. She tucked herself in my blankie, brushing her body against mine. Seeing her do that, I panicked and immediately disconnected the call.

Naina and I kept staring at each other for what seemed like an eternity. Even though I was completely and heartily enjoying the moment, a small part of me was wishing for Rahul to call and interrupt all the sexual tension between us. But he didn't call, and after all that staring that was only getting lacy by the second, I couldn't control myself.

We were now breathing into each other in complete silence. As I continued to stare at her hair blow every so often when the blades of the air-conditioner would point at her, I couldn't help but admire the beauty of her pale cheeks.

'Remember the day, we were looking at each other as you walked through the college gates?' I murmured in a slow, heavy tone.

Naina nodded.

'I've never stopped thinking about you, about the magic of how we met.'

Naina nodded again with a hint of blush.

I pecked on Naina's cheek, and said, 'You're very beautiful and I'll always treat you as the most beautiful thing in this world.'

Naina, who hadn't spoken a word since the big reveal, tightly held my hand.

'*Doofie,*' she mumbled.

'Yup.'

'Do it again.'

'What?'

'The kiss, duh!'

'*Ayio.*'

'But…'

'Umm?'

'This time on my lips.'

And just as she finished her sentence, I held Naina by her waist, making her rest on top of me. With the only thing between us being the heavy, and yet comforting blankie, I brushed my fingers against Naina's hair, and just when she turned her eyes towards my playful fingers, I locked my lips onto her lips, making our souls unite into one.

'You! Sir… are a very good kisser,' Naina mumbled.

My lips, which had been gracing every ounce of Naina's sweet taste, were now working their way towards her neck, and as I continued to trace the sensitive parts of her curves, she couldn't help but moan in all the excitement.

In the heat of the moment, what we didn't realize was that we had never locked the door, as we weren't used to locking it, and once Naina's moans started to gain pace, it wasn't much longer before my mother barged into my room. And even then, it wasn't until my mother tried separating us, did we realize that we weren't alone.

Naina immediately sprang up from the bed and stood in one of the corners with her head faced down in shame. My mother grabbed hold of my hand and dragged me out of the bed, pulling me towards her. She signaled at Naina to leave, but Naina knew that leaving me alone with my mother wasn't going to be safe, so, she chose to stand beside me instead, and gracefully took hold of my hand.

'Naina! Leave!' my mother yelled.

But Naina wasn't the one to listen. Instead, she inched closer to me.

'Your father and I are spending so much money on your treatment and you're wasting your life like this?' my mother continued. 'Don't you have any shame?'

'You're the reason he went into that coma,' Naina gushed.

I pressed onto Naina's hands, signaling her to stop.

'I've been listening to all your taunts for a long time, and even though you keep saying I am the culprit, I haven't quite figured out as to why I am one,' I said, looking my mother in the eye.

'You don't?' my mother asked.

'Please! Enlighten me!'

'You're the reason I am in this mess!'

'What mess?'

'When's your birthday?'

'Next Month.'

'And when's my anniversary?'

'It was five months ago.'

'Get it?'

'Get what?'

Naina who had been holding my hand tight all this while, suddenly let it go. She turned towards me, and for some strange reason, hugged me tightly.

'You think your father's the man of my dreams? Do you think I went against my family for the sake of love? Do you think that from aspiring to be a role model to millions, I deliberately chose to be stuck with a ten-year older nobody? You think love unites us all?'

All this while, Naina still hadn't let go of me, and even though I was beginning to realize the reason behind my mother's cruel behavior towards me, I was still far from coming to any conclusion.

'I had one stupid fling before my big break in life, and the next thing I know, I was being forced to marry my mistake, only so that my family could save its precious pride. I don't hate you. I try my best to love you, but you keep reminding me of the life I could have had, had it not been for you, and that's the only reason that I am so harsh on you.'

A tear rolled down my cheek. A billion thoughts were now crossing my mind. It felt like, I should have said something, but I just didn't know what to say. I let go of Naina, as I continued to stare blankly at my mother.

'And this father of yours? You think he's a saint, don't you? Do you think he's got all the qualities of a gentleman? Naina! I am warning you, if *Doofie* is anything like his father, you better stay far away from him.'

'But I am as much like you as I am like father,' I stammered.

'I can't even imagine what you must be going through, but taking it all out on Doofus isn't the solution,' Naina said.

'Then who do I take it out on? My husband, who's been molesting me since the day I've known him? My mother, who won't listen to me because I am her daughter and not her son? Or my father who still hasn't forgiven me for my mistake? Or do I take it out on you?'

• • •

Naina didn't respond.

'I know I'm bad, but only because the world around me has made me so, and in all my lashing out at *Doofie,* I keep hoping that maybe, he'll realize the pain behind all that anger, but this so-called family of his has painted such a fairyland picture in his mind, that he can never fathom the truth.'

As my mother kept speaking, the delusion that I had invented for myself was now becoming clear. All her fake waves of laughter, all those hitting that my father used to laugh off as being playful, all those tortures were becoming evident now. I had never really understood why my uncle's family had suddenly started living with us a month ago, but now I could see why. Heck! My father didn't even come to the hospital when I was in a coma, and when people said he was extremely busy, I had gladly accepted it. All of a sudden, a shiver went down my spine, and within moments, I dropped to the floor, unconscious.

I could hear the voice of Naina screaming inside my head, or it was the doctor, I don't really know. And for some strange reason, they were yelling *CUT.* Suddenly, I felt my entire body shake again, and I could feel as if water was being splashed at me. When moments later, I finally opened my eyes, Naina and Utkarsh were staring at me dressed in a fancy sort of attire.

'You were supposed to pretend to be dead and not actually die,' Utkarsh said and began laughing.

• • •

'Did you doze off?' Naina asked playfully slapping my face.

It was then, that I realized that we had been rehearsing for the college play, and I was playing a dead person. I was awake now, but I was too disturbed at what my stupid mind had made me go through. I stood upon the stage, and without saying a word, I started walking and left.

ΔΔΔ

Super Child

'Why am I dark-skinned, daddy?' I whined.

'And why do you care?' My father asked, still busy staring at the television.

'Because my friends make fun of me,' I said.

'Why? Cause they are fairer than you?'

I nodded.

'They say they are better than me because they have whiter skin,' I gushed.

My father switched the television off and turned towards me. He handed me his smartphone and said, 'Search for *the color of defeat* on Google for me, will you?'

I immediately long pressed the home button making *Google Assistant* pop-up.

'Ok Google! What is the color of defeat?' I asked.

According to the search results, A white flag is used to indicate defeat during a fight or a war.

Just then, my silver bracelet started to glow. It

wasn't too bright, in fact, even if my father was staring hard at it, he wouldn't have noticed it. Realizing that someone was in danger, I immediately flung the phone on the sofa and ran off to my room.

'Where are you going kiddo?' my father called behind me.

But I didn't stop. It took me a second to change into my costume, and once I locked in the coordinates of the place I was headed for, I closed my eyes and made one fast swirl.

'Why fear when *Doofie is here,*' I exclaimed, as I made my magical appearance between two distinctive hoomans inside of a moving train.

From the looks of it, the person behind me – This little girl was probably the one in danger, and the kid in front of me – A short and chubby boy was the one who was going to get his tummy kicked.

'*Doofie,* you're here!' the girl cheered.

'Yes, little girl,' I continued, 'Is this boy bothering you?'

'He says, he wants to eat me,' the girl whined, pointing a finger at the boy.

'She called me fat,' the boy said.

'You are fat!' the girl said.

'You're stupid.'

'No, you're stupid!'

I was patiently looking at the two of them fight like kids when my bracelet began to glow again. Well, in their defense, they, in fact, were kids, and it was going to be a while before they stopped this pointless name-calling, and considering that my bracelet was radiating a bluish aura rather than the bright yellow, I absolutely needed to go. So, I closed my eyes and made a big swirl.

'Do you need my help?' I asked my mother.

'Can you call your father? These pots are stuck together and won't come apart,' my mother said.

'I'll help you,' I said.

My mother looked at me and waved her hands over my head.

'Are we playing superhero today? Call your father, these pots are heavy,' she said.

And that's when I realized that I had forgotten to change my costume. Nonetheless, I took the steel pots from my mother's hand, and slowly rotated them bringing them apart. When I was done, I handed them to my mother and without waiting for her reaction, I ran off to my room, and then back to the train.

'You're *Paneer*.' (Cottage cheese.)

'I am not *Paneer*.'

'*Paneer?*'

'*Doofie!* Where did you go?' the girl asked.

'Who's *Paneer?*' I asked.

'She is,' the boy said.

'I'm not *Paneer!* I'm Palak.' The girl continued, 'And he's a hippopotamus.'

I turned towards the boy waiting for him to say something, but he stayed mum, and within a second, a tear rolled down his cheek.

'Hippo is crying! Hippo is crying,' Palak began to tease.

And the next thing I know, the chubby kid sat down on the train's floor and began to cry his heart out.

Waaaaaaaaaaa

'Who made my kid cry?' A female voice emerged from a distance.

The lady who was yelling was probably the kid's mother and must have been standing on the narrow passage of the train's compartment. She stopped just beside her kid and looked at us with a strange kind of glare.

'Who made him cry?' the lady asked.

'He did!' Palak said, instantly pointing her finger at me.

'Thanks much, eh?' I said throwing my hands up in the air.

'*Sollie...*' Palak mumbled.

By this time, the bully's father had also arrived on the scene. He picked his son up and began to dust the dirt off the back of his pants. The kid who had now stopped crying looked at me and then at Palak. Palak saw him looking at her and stuck her tongue out to tease him. Now, I don't know if he got scared or if he didn't care anymore, because the kid just turned around and ran off.

'I am sorry. I could have stopped his crying,' I said

to the kid's mother.

'And why are you dressed like this?' the mother asked.

'Because...'

'He's a superhero,' Palak cheered.

The mother looked at both of us and shrugged.

'Aren't we all?' she said and left after her kid.

The father followed suit.

'Why did you rat me out?' I asked Palak.

'I was giving you a chance to save me,' she said.

'Wow! You're impossible.'

'No! I'm Palak,' she cheered.

'As in the Spinach?'

Palak raised her burrows and pouted.

'Huh! Palak as in the eye-lashes.'

Now that Palak and I were alone, I was finally able to notice her. She was about the same height as I was and was wearing a pinkish Kurti with a flower brooch that was beautifully complimenting her dress. She had a teeny-weeny *bindi* on her forehead and a set of large *jhumkas* hung on her ears. And to complete the entire attire, she had a green colored *dupatta* hanging out one of the sides of her shoulder. All of this packed into a body that was no more than four and a half feet made her absolutely look adorable. But she wasn't adorable, was she?

'What you did to that kid wasn't cool,' I gushed, looking straight at Palak.

'I know,' she said.

• • •

'And… Wait, what?'

Choo-Choo

'I get down over here, I have to perform at the theatre today,' Palak said.

'Oh! Wow!'

'If you have time, come see my performance, *Doofie.*' She said and smiled.

I didn't have my answer, and I didn't think I was going to get it at that moment. And most importantly, when Palak invited me to her performance, she did it with such cuteness, that I couldn't say no. But then, I noticed the movements outside the window and facepalmed.

'The whistle was for the train to leave little girl,' I said, pointing outside with my hands.

Palak rushed to look out of the window, and then she rushed towards the gate, but by the time she reached the gate, the train had already picked up pace.

She returned back to where I was, with a sullen face and took a seat.

'What do I do now? I don't know my way,' she said.

'Serves you right,' I said, sitting on the berth in front of her.

'Why *Doofie?*'

'You made that kid cry, remember?'

'I didn't mean to… I was just teasing him.'

'But it did hurt him, *na.*'

'I am *sollie…* I didn't know,' Palak continued, 'Can

you help me reach the theatre?'

'Only if you promise me that you won't make fun of people anymore.'

Palak looked at me wide-eyed and nodded.

'Grab my hand then and close your eyes... I'll fly you to your venue.'

'What if I fall?'

'You won't, duh.'

'What if you fall?' Palak asked, tightly holding both my hands.

'You know, everyone's a dreamer and everyone's a superhero. It doesn't matter who you are or how you look, you're all capable of achieving great things. But that is only going to be possible if you look at all the negativity in the eye, and not let it affect you. People will call you names, they will make fun of your body, they might even judge you on your character, and when they do, let them. Because, if someone is going all the way to notice your pointless quirks, it should only make you feel special. There's a reason negativity exists in this world, and that is because most people don't realize that they are being negative. People need to be taught; they need to be educated...'

Palak reached for her bag and took out a pack of *Frootie*. She took a long sip as she continued being an audience to my speech, but with an expressionless face.

'You didn't get a word that I said, did you?'

Palak shook her head and smiled.

• • •

So, I silently waited for her to finish her *Frootie,* and when she was done, I made her hold my hand and we swirled our way to the theatre.

'Will you come to see my performance?' Palak asked.

'Yup,' I said.

'Come without the mask, okay? And maybe I'll recognize you.'

Palak stepped closer towards me and gave a peck on my cheek. She, then, turned around and galloped inside the theatre like an angel.

'Why fear when *Doofie* is here,' I mumbled to myself and made a swirl for my home.

⋆Kaboom⋆

'Are you okay?'

'Shit! He's bleeding.'

'Help! Is someone on this train a doctor? My kid's hurt his head.'

'Yes… I am. What happened?'

'He fell off the middle berth and is now bleeding.'

'Let me take a look!'

'Will he be okay, doctor?'

'Yes, the bleeding has stopped. Let's just hope he doesn't suffer from any brain damage.'

'Will he?'

'Not likely, what's his name?'

'Doofus.'

ΔΔΔ

• • •

The Idea [Bonus]

I cannot believe that it's been so long since the time I met all these people, who had an impact on my life. The journey that has led me up to this moment has been a bag of mixed emotions. For a while, I had thought that all was lost, but then out of nowhere, a new set of people emerged and it's been a smooth sail, at least for most of the parts. And the funny thing is, that while I sit here and think about how I could have changed everything that has happened to me, I realize, that it all happened for a reason, and the idea behind that reason has finally become clear to me.

But, now comes the hard part, for I need to reconcile with the people I have lost, I need to go down the memory lane with people who choose not to remember me, and the funniest of all, I need to finally face the people who think that I am worth something.

Now, I may be stupid, or maybe I flatter myself,

but I know that when you knock on the door of someone who doesn't want anything to do with you, the response is only going to be a cold one. I also know that when you think about all the sacrifices you made and realize that you didn't really need to make them, people will be sure to point that out.

Obviously, I had to start from where it all began. Because this person and the time that I spent with her was the defining moment of my life. So, the first person I thought of calling was none other than Rhea herself, but, for some strange reason, my call went into a cross-connection. Now, that's okay, telephone companies are known to fuck up in moments like these, and I was expecting to be talking to some sixty-year-old Brazilian beauty. But no, the call instead got connected to my next-door neighbor; Tania, and after we had a very awkward talk about this life in general, I eventually ended up inviting her. Then, I called Rhea again.

Surprisingly, the call went smooth, and after we briefly relived our memories, I popped her the question, and she agreed to meet me.

I also tried getting in touch with Fuck-boy, who initially had his doubts, but once I tricked him into believing that he was going to get a lot of screen time, even he agreed to meet me.

When I look back at a time, when I wasn't sure what I wanted to do with my life, I always blame it on my inability to complete something. I've had my hands on so many things, and have done them all with such enthusiasm, but every time, it's time to cross the finish line, I always end up making a U-turn and start racing in the opposite direction. So, when this idea struck me, and every cell of my body was more than willing to finish this race, I couldn't even believe myself.

The easiest part was to convince my friends. I didn't even take an initiative to call them. I simply left a message on our dead WhatsApp group, and they were instantly ready for it.

There are moments when you think about how big a dreamer you used to be in your childhood. How you were affected by the silliest of things and yet, you weren't affected by the trivial ones. The present me might have settled on most of my childhood dreams, but a few significant ones out of those were still alive, and even though, I couldn't possibly bring that dreamer child back, I had decided it in my heart that I would think of him when I presented my idea.

I know, I invited my friends and I didn't even give any special preference to that one friend who had now become so much more. Well, in my defense, she had been trivial in my going through with this decision, and she already knew about it for a long time.

I had been doing all of this from my office, and that meant, that my colleagues obviously were noticing that I was inviting people to some big event.

'What's the party about?' My colleague asked.

This was the same guy who had taken me and my father to the *Dhongi Baba,* and there was no chance I was going to reveal my idea to someone who believed in superstitions. I simply shrugged and ignored my colleague's question.

The next part was the hardest, and it required a butt load of courage for me to go through with it. In fact, this one was so hard that I kept delaying it, for as long as I could. Eventually, I knew that it had to be done. So, I took a deep breath and finally went live on social media to invite the thousands of fans that I had over there. After all, these were the people who had directly contributed to this idea. They were my constant support, and even though, they might not know it, but they have always meant a lot to me. And when all of them agreed to be there, I couldn't have been happier.

'*Doofie,*' Naina texted, 'You love me, no?'

This was after I had turned the live-video off, and I had been too tired to talk anymore. So, I just laid down on my bed, with my phone kept to the side. Obviously, I loved her, and not just because she was beautiful… I loved her because she completed me in every possible way. But as I said, this was after my live-video, so maybe I needed some alone time, or maybe I had subconsciously dozed off, but I didn't respond.

And the next thing I know, Naina showed up at my door with a cute little puppy. She had bought the puppy in both our names as a symbol of our innocent and cute love.

We played with the puppy for a while and then, I asked her if she was okay with me inviting the college rep for the event. At first, she nodded, but then she began to behave so weirdly, that I had to eventually drop the rep from my list.

We then sat down to decide on the venue for the event, and after going through numerous choices, we were down to two. We could either have the event at the floating hotel on the *Hooghly river,* or we could do it in an open park under the charm of the Moon.

'You know, if we do it on the hotel's deck like rooftop, we get the anxiousness of the river waves as well as the nostalgia of the moon,' Naina exclaimed.

And with that, the venue for the event got finalized.

'We'll use *eco-friendly* cutlery and maybe, we can have *halwa* and *samosa* on the menu,' I said to Naina and made her in-charge of conveying the same to the caterer.

It had gotten late by that time and Naina had to rush back home. We shared a passionate kiss, and then I dropped her home.

'What about your parents?' She asked while getting down the car.

'They'll obviously be there,' I said and smiled.

I watched her go inside her apartment, and, then I drove back home.

• • •

The event; the reunion; the nostalgia, the big reveal of the idea – it was supposed to happen seven days from now and the fact that I had managed to handle everything with such ease made me feel no less than a *Superhero*. Everything felt so surreal and things were happening so fast, that it felt like I'd miss all of it even if I blinked my eyes. And speaking about eyes, I was so nervous about it, that I had already wished upon two of my broken eye-lashes in this past one week.

The gates for the event opened on time. And the guests started pouring in right after that. Of course, my friends were here since the morning, and we had more than made sure that things were set up according to the plan.

There was going to be a special row in the front, comprising of all the people my idea revolved around. Moreover, the middle two seats of that row were going to have two special people who were going to play a major role in the completion of my idea – Kalpana and Shobhana. And finally, from the second row, all my peeps from Instagram were going to sit.

It was almost an hour before everyone was to arrive on the deck. My cousin was the last to arrive on the scene and the weird thing was that I didn't even recall inviting him.

I peeked out from the backstage and I swear, the deck had more people than on the Titanic. I took a deep long breath and finally took center stage.

• • •

For a moment, the entire deck went silent, but then, one of them stood up, and then another, and then another, and just like that, the entire audience was clapping and giving me a standing ovation even before I had presented my idea.

Everyone in the front row was quickly given a pencil and a pad – for they were to jot down points about my speech, that could potentially help them reach a decision.

'Hi! I am Doofus, and I suffer from *Sleep Paralysis* and *Vivid Dreams Syndrome*… This means that I see dreams – dreams that feel so real that they can make you question your reality,' I said.

Someone from the crowd hooted, and even though I hadn't said anything significant yet, Fuck-boy had already begun scribbling on his notepad.

'Over the years, I have seen quite a many dreams, and some way or the other, you people have been an integral part of it,' I continued, 'So, in a way, you guys are the major investors of this new journey that I plan to take.'

There was another round of cheer, and by now, most of my special guests were writing something.

'What's this journey about?' Rhea asked.

'It's about you, it's about me, it's a book about all of us.'

'Is it about the Moon?' someone from the crowd asked and then raised her hands.

I nodded.

'So, who all are going to be a part of this journey and help me turn this book based on my dreams into a reality?' I asked scanning the entire room.

'I am in,' my mother yelled from her seat.

'I am in,' Naina said from the backstage.

'I am also in,' Rahul said, who was standing just beside Naina.

And within seconds, almost everyone was chanting *'I am in!'* in unison.

'Wait!' Tania cried, 'What's going to be the name of this book?'

I looked at her, and for some strange reason, she was dressed like a princess. Seeing her dressed like that brought an instant smile on my face.

'Paralyzed in Dreamland,' I said.

ΔΔΔ

Author's Note: This bonus story contains lines and references from all the previous stories. How many of those Easter eggs could you find?

Now that you've finished reading this book, I know that you have this question, and yes, all the stories were actual dreams. If you liked this concept and liked the stories, please do drop a text on Instagram. It would also mean a lot to me if you left a review on Amazon or Flipkart – depending on where you bought the book from. And yes, the most important, yet heartbreaking part of any book – The End.